Where's Jim Now?

Where's Jim Now?

Bianca Bradbury

Houghton Mifflin Company Boston 1978

Library of Congress Cataloging in Publication Data

Bradbury, Bianca.
  Where's Jim now?

  SUMMARY: When Dave's half-brother joins the
family after spending time in a rehabilitation
institute, he seems unable to stay out of trouble.
  [1. Brothers and sisters—Fiction] I. Title.
PZ7.B716Wh   [Fic]   78-14832
ISBN 0-395-27160-6

Also by Bianca Bradbury

Andy's Mountain
Dogs and More Dogs
"I'm Vinny, I'm Me"
In Her Father's Footsteps
Jim and His Monkey
The Loner
Mutt
My Pretty Girl
A New Penny
One Kitten Too Many
The Three Keys
Those Traver Kids
Two on an Island

Where's Jim Now?

1

DAVE LINGERED on the dock, making sure everything was shipshape. A neighbor, Mr. Richter, had helped Dave haul out the twelve small rowboats, which were now arranged in a neat line along the beach, bottoms up. The raft was tucked under the dock. The fishing lodge was ready for the long winter, wasn't it? Dave was the man of the family now, and it was up to him to make sure.

He wasn't lingering really; he was stalling. The lodge was a silent place now, without his father's booming laugh echoing through it. His mother was doing her best, and her best was very good; but the loss of his father was like a dull pain in Dave's ribs that never went away.

Now, in early November, dusk came early. Seeing lights at the end of the lane, Dave walked down to fetch the newspaper. The Harrisons lived so far from town, the paper was delivered by car and left in the mailbox.

The *Northford News* might have some sort of a story that would give him and his mother something to talk about at supper. They couldn't talk about loneliness, so they were grateful for any interesting items in the paper.

He pushed open the kitchen door, entering the brightly lit kitchen. Beth Harrison was just taking baked potatoes and a meatloaf out of the oven. "Hey," Dave said, "that smells neat."

"You got the paper. I thought I saw the lights."

They sat down and helped themselves to the salad and hot food. "This is great," Dave said. He added, trying to make conversation like the man of the house, "How was your day?"

His mother smiled, and that made her look younger. It was hard for Dave to realize that nowadays she was actually a high school teacher. "It was a day," she said. "I'm getting used to it. When I first started I felt as though I was walking into a den of lions, but maybe the lions are getting friendlier. I can see they're nice lions."

"You were really scared."

"I was really scared," she agreed. "But still, I couldn't believe my good luck that I got such a job, right off, at our own Regional High. Teaching history, too, and that was always my favorite subject."

The evening paper lay beside Dave's place, and

Beth added, "Go ahead, look. See what's happening in the world."

He spread out the paper. "They voted to build a sewer system in Northford," he told her.

"That's not exactly fascinating, but I'm glad we don't live there. I'd hate to have to pay the assessment." The Harrisons lived in Hobb Creek, a tiny town twenty miles from Northford.

"Lew Collins's sister is going to get married."

"That's nice. I hope he's a nice boy."

Dave read a small item on the front page, bent closer, read it again. His face must have changed because his mother asked, "What is it, Dave?"

"Here's a funny one," he said. "It's about a boy named James Harrison, only maybe he's a man, the paper doesn't say. He stole a car in Northford and was arrested. The paper says he couldn't put up bond so he's in jail awaiting trial."

"James Harrison. The paper doesn't give his age?"

"No."

"It could be our Jim."

"How could it? Jimmy doesn't steal cars!" Dave exclaimed.

His mother said gently, "How do we know, Dave? We haven't seen him since — how long? I think it was at least five years ago, the last time he visited us. Then he just dropped out of sight, and that worried your dad dreadfully."

"What can we do?" Dave asked. "I mean, what are we supposed to do?"

"I don't know," she said. "The names being the same, that bothers me."

She got up and cleared the table, poured coffee for herself, and brought Dave milk and cookies. "I think we'll have to find out," she said. "I just couldn't rest easy, never knowing."

The kitchen phone had a long cord, so she brought it to the table, looked up the Northford Police Department, and dialed the number. She asked the man who answered if he could give her information about an arrest made the day before. "A person named James Harrison," she said. "Is he blond or dark? How old is he?"

Her face paled. "He's nineteen and he's light-haired. Could you ask him one question. Does he know the Joseph Harrison family in Hobb Creek?"

The officer did as she asked, and when he returned to the phone she said, "All right, Sergeant Noonan, thank you very much."

She absently stirred her coffee. "This boy claims he doesn't know any Joseph Harrisons in Hobb Creek," she told Dave.

"Just the same, this thing bugs you," Dave commented, watching her.

"That's right," she admitted. "I mean, there are too many coincidences. There's the name, and the age, and the fact that the sergeant said he was not a local boy."

She seemed to give herself a mental shake. "Let's forget about it," she said. "You have homework to do, and I have papers to correct."

Dave helped with the dishes and then went to his room to tackle his homework. When he finished it, he rejoined his mother and they watched a movie on TV for a while, but it was a stupid movie and they turned it off and went to bed.

Dave didn't sleep well. He spent most of the night thrashing around on his bed under the eaves. Once he started up, fully awake, and it seemed as though a question was sitting there on the foot of his bed. Was his own half brother the James Harrison who had been busted in Northford for swiping a car?

Lying in the dark, Dave tried to sort out the facts. What did he know about Jim? Not much, really. Jim was the only child of Joseph Harrison's first marriage, which had ended in divorce. His first wife, Nina, had gotten custody of the boy. Dave himself was the only child of his father's second marriage, and that was a really happy marriage, with the three of them — Joe and Beth and Dave — sharing a lot of love.

That was why Joseph Harrison's death had come as such an awful, nasty shock. Dave deliberately pushed away the memory. Even now, four months later, he still wasn't ready to really look at it. He went back to thinking about Jim.

Nina had let Jim come and visit, once in a while, although she had moved far away. The last time was five years ago, when Dave was nine. Jim was fourteen, but he and Dave had had a wonderful time together, as though they were the same age. Jim had lived with them here at Journey's End, the fishing lodge, and had seemed to be completely happy. He hadn't said so, but Dave had gotten the impression that Jim's life with his mother was miserable. Nina had remarried, and Jim didn't like his stepfather.

All of this was vague in Dave's mind because it had happened so long ago, but he did remember the day they drove Jim to Northford, to take a plane back to his "real" life. Jim wasn't laughing that day. Dave was sitting up front with his father, and he had turned around and seen that Beth's arm was around Jim, and Jim was crying on her shoulder. The sight of a fourteen-year-old boy crying had shocked Dave so, he never forgot it.

They reached the airport, and Jim still didn't have control over himself. After his father bought his ticket he clutched each of them, hugging them, and muttered, "I'll be back. I've got to come back." Then he bolted down the ramp to the gate and his plane.

They watched it take off, and Dave's mother said, "I really love that boy, Joe."

Dave succeeded in blotting out that old memory, and slept. When morning came, though, he felt tired, worn out before the new day even began. He dragged himself downstairs.

His mother was in the kitchen. She fixed breakfast and they sat together at the table, but she only poked at her food. Her eyes had dark shadows under them. "You're still bugged about that piece in the paper," Dave said.

"That's true," she admitted. "I simply cannot put it out of my mind. Dave, we've got to see that boy. If we don't we'll wonder forever after, was it our Jim or wasn't it? Suppose you don't take the school bus home today. I'll pick you up as soon as my last class is over, and we'll go to Northford."

"Okay, that suits me fine," Dave told her.

"Because he could be your brother."

"Right," Dave said, and he was very much relieved.

He waited outside that afternoon, watching for the old station wagon. His school was on Main Street in Hobb Creek, and the regional high school was out in the country. His mother drove up and he hopped in.

She started, "Do you remember?" as soon as they were on their way to Northford. "Do you remember Jim's raccoon?" she asked. "That was a long time ago, but I'll bet you never forgot that raccoon either. What did he call it? Herman. Jim was sleeping in the room off the kitchen, and it used to come to his window in the evenings and watch him. Pretty soon he made friends with it, and before long it was in the bedroom. Until that awful night when it got hold of a feather pillow and tore it up. Do you remember the mess? I thought we'd never see the last of those feathers!"

Dave laughed. "Sure I remember Herman!"

"He only came a couple of times after Jim left. Then we never saw him again."

They rode awhile. Then Beth said, "Oh dear," and stopped the car. She turned to Dave. "I've just realized something rather awful," she said. "Jim doesn't know his father is dead. We'll have to tell him." She sat thinking for a moment. Then she said, "But maybe it isn't our Jim. It can't be. Our Jim would never steal a car."

Dave had no answer to that. They went on.

They had never been to the police station in Northford and had a little trouble locating it on a side street. Another officer was at the desk, and he knew nothing of Beth's call the night before. He summoned the chief, whose name was Parcells, and Beth explained.

"Court was held this morning," Chief Parcells told her. "There was no argument over the facts; Harrison admitted the theft. He received an indeterminate sentence to the Burrows Rehabilitation Institute. One of the officers is driving him there, and they're just about ready to leave."

"Could we see the boy?" Beth asked.

"I don't see why not. At least you can, ma'am, but I don't know about your son."

"Please," Beth said. "If this is our James Harrison, then he's Dave's half brother."

"All right," the chief said, and led them to his private office.

While they waited Dave was studying his mother. He was surprised by her courage, and that was the truth. He had seen plenty of it while his father was so ill, and when his father died and she had faced up to an uncertain, lonely future. But this was another kind of courage she was showing, marching into a police station, asking favors, when she had never in her whole life had anything to do with the law. This situation probably scared her as much as it scared Dave.

The chief was back. "I can only give you a few minutes, Mrs. Harrison," he said. "The officer who's taking the boy to B.R.I. can't wait any longer than that." He stepped aside. "Here he is."

Jim was in the doorway. Yes, it was their Jim, five years older, but with the same open, friendly face, the same broad shoulders, the same unruly mane of sandy hair. He wasn't wearing handcuffs or anything like that. He just stood there until the chief left, closing the door. Then he smiled, but his smile was uncertain, and he said, "Hey, what are you doing here? Where's Dad?"

Beth said, her voice high but steady, "Your father died last spring. I'm so sorry to have to tell you, Jim."

"No! How could he? What was it?"

"Cancer."

Jim grabbed Beth and held her close. Finally he let her go and blew his nose. "You shouldn't have come here," he said.

"We had to," Beth told him. "Dave read about your arrest in the paper. Why didn't you come home, when you were so close?"

"I didn't think it was my home," he replied.

"Of course it is!"

Dave tried a new angle. "What about this Burrows Rehabilitation Institute, where you're going?" he asked.

Jim turned to him. "It's okay, Davey. I've been there before. I was let out two, three months ago. I've got friends there."

"We didn't even know you were in this state," Dave said.

"Where's your mother?" Beth asked.

"I don't know," Jim told her and he sounded bitter. "She's got another new husband. I think maybe she's in New Orleans."

Chief Parcells opened the door then. "The officer will have to take Jim now," he announced.

Jim got to his feet, seeming relieved by the interruption. "Let's go!" he said, and started for the door.

"No, wait!" Beth ordered. "Jim, whether you want to see us or not, we can't let you just disappear. We'll be in touch."

Jim turned back and put his arms around her. Dave came only to his shoulder, and was suddenly smothered in a bear hug. "Good-bye, little brother," Jim said, and bolted out the door.

They stood at the window, forlornly watching.

11

The officer put the cuffs on Jim and helped him into the back seat of the patrol car, which had a wire partition for the driver's protection. Jim was studying the windows of the police station and, seeing them, lifted the cuffs in a good-bye gesture. He was trying to grin, and he watched out the back window as the car drove away.

Dave's mother was frankly crying. Dave just wanted out, and he said, "Come on, Mom." This place scared him, and he wanted to get away and go home.

It wasn't that easy. "Please sit down," Chief Parcells said. "I have Jim's file here. I'd like to talk to you about the case, Mrs. Harrison."

2

THE CHIEF set chairs for them facing his desk. "Frankly, I don't know where to begin," he said. Dave was surprised; this middle-aged, pleasant cop seemed really concerned about the prisoner who had just departed.

"This case has us all puzzled," the chief went on. "Jim made very little effort to avoid arrest. He was walking along Main Street and spotted a car that had keys in the ignition, so he got in and drove around town for a little while. The owner saw him take off, and told the officer who was directing traffic at the corner of Maple Street, and the officer brought her here to make out a report. We sent a squad car to look for him, and the officers found him sitting in the stolen car, right on Main Street.

"We checked back on his record and found out he had done the same thing in a town at the other side of the state. I mean, he stole a car and drove around for a while, but didn't leave town. They had no choice any more than we did: they had to arrest him, because theft is theft. In your opinion, is the boy retarded, Mrs. Harrison? I'm asking because his making so little effort to avoid arrest is so peculiar."

That question startled Dave, and he waited for his mother's answer. "I don't believe Jim is retarded," she said. "I knew him when he was younger, and I never saw any evidence. If my husband had, I'm sure he would have spoken about it. His mother had full custody of him. After my husband was divorced from Nina, his first wife, he paid support for the boy, of course. He engaged a lawyer who tried to get the court to grant Joe full custody of his son, but the court refused. Then Nina and Jim disappeared for long periods. She allowed Jim to come for visits with us, a few times."

Chief Parcells consulted the file. "His mother had him committed to Moorhaven, an institution for the retarded."

"When was that?"

"Three years ago, when the boy was sixteen. This case intrigued me, so I put in a call and got the Moorhaven records. They had found no evidence of retardation. He's a troubled boy, that's clear, but there's no indication of mental deficiency. At Moorhaven they trained him to rebuild motors, and found

14

he was good at that, almost a genius. They got him a job, and he lived on his own for a time. Then he was arrested for car theft, as I just told you.

"He was sent to Burrows Rehab, and his record there is a good one. They discharged him a few months ago. Apparently he drifted around for a while, and then came here, and you know the rest."

Dave thought the chief was finished, but he wasn't. "This thing bothers me," he said. "I suppose if we had a psychologist, he or she might make something of it, but in a town this size we can't afford to hire one. We just do the best we can, and the best thing seemed to be to send him back to Burrows. The boy seemed to welcome that decision."

Beth and Dave waited, but Chief Parcells didn't go on, so they thanked him and left.

They started home. Both were thinking deeply, and finally Dave turned to his mother. "Mom, what did the chief mean when he said Jim was troubled?"

"Well, how could he help but be? He must have had a really rough life with Nina. That bothered your Dad terribly, but there was absolutely nothing he could do about it because she had custody."

They were halfway home when they saw a steak house ahead, and Beth turned in. "Can we afford a fancy dinner?" Dave asked.

"Yes," Beth said. "We've got to put this thing

15

out of our minds. Jimmy's gone, and there's not much we can do for him, except to write letters to him. If we have a pleasant dinner, perhaps that will help us. It will be some kind of break between us and this horrible day." Dave didn't argue.

The food at the steak house was great. Dave and his mother talked about that; they didn't mention Jim.

Dave didn't really succeed in putting his half brother out of his mind, though. After he was in bed that night, that last picture came back to him, Jim in the cop's car searching the police station windows for a glimpse of them, trying to smile and wave his cuffed hands.

There was a little envy mixed in with Dave's feeling about his brother. Jim looked just like their father. Why couldn't Dave be big too, and broad-shouldered and good-looking? Dave wasn't exactly a shrimp, but he was never going to make six feet four. And Jim was a natural athlete like Joe Harrison, while Dave was lousy at sports. Well, maybe not lousy, but mediocre.

Dave finally shook off that line of thought, and slept.

His mother didn't speak of the incident the next morning, and neither did he. It came up again, however, at school. After lunch the boys were tossing a football around on the macadam parking lot, trying to keep warm against the November chill. They gave that up and gathered at the door, waiting for the bell. Lewis Collins, Dave's best friend, spoke about it. "We read in the paper about a kid being arrested in Northford for swiping a car," he told Dave. "My dad mentioned that you had a brother with the same name."

Lew had kept his voice low, but the others heard and were waiting for Dave's answer. Dave was suddenly very uptight, and didn't think fast enough to lie. "Yeah," he said.

"Yeah?" Bert Warden demanded.

"It was Jim Harrison, only he isn't really my brother," Dave explained. "He's a half brother. I mean, my father was married once to his mother."

All the boys were interested, as they'd be interested in anybody who had a brother who had been busted by the cops, but the bell saved Dave. He and Lew separated from the others, taking the corridor that led to the sections of the eighth grade. Lew paused outside 41, their homeroom. "I'm sorry," he said. "I shouldn't have brought that up in front of the other guys."

"That's okay," Dave said. "My mother and I

went over to Northford to see him." Their teacher was at the door telling them to hurry up, so again Dave was rescued from a tricky conversation.

Lew wasn't a bus kid — he lived in Hobb Creek — but after school he waited with Dave while the buses were assembling. Dave was hoping he had forgotten the whole thing, but no such luck. Lew brought it up again. He didn't want to talk about Jim, though. He asked a lot of questions about what Dave had seen and heard at the police station.

Dave didn't mention any of this to his mother when he arrived home, and she didn't mention Jim, either. Both seemed to want to drop the subject.

Life was hard enough, without any extra problems. Getting along without a husband and father, weathering through a northern winter in an enormous old fishing lodge — these presented enough problems.

The Harrisons had lived in a nice little house in Hobb Creek where Joe Harrison had a good job as boss of a crew for the power company. Then Dave's grandfather had died, leaving Journey's End to his only son. The family had always spent their summers there, and Joe got the idea they ought to live there year 'round.

It was a huge barn of a place, twenty-five bedrooms, six baths, a game room, and a big dining room. The owner's quarters were in the ell. Joe wanted to keep his job with the power company, and in his spare time fix up the place and reopen it, winterizing the ell as a comfortable home for Beth and Dave and himself.

The family had gone along with this idea. Dave was delighted, because he had loved his grandfather and he loved the ramshackle lodge. Beth wasn't so crazy about the idea but she *was* crazy about Joe Harrison, so she agreed. They sold the house in town and moved. Then Joe got sick, and then with terrible swiftness he was suddenly very sick, and died.

So here they were. The ell wasn't winterized, nothing was ready. They had rented boats last summer so local people could fish in Enoch's Pond. Dave, with the help of Mr. Richter, down the road, had hauled the boats up on the beach, but that was all that had been done.

Journey's End was a difficult place to live in. As for business, it couldn't possibly be run by one boy and a woman who had had to take a full-time job in order to earn a living. Dave and Beth had a very big question to face: Should they sell? They couldn't make a decision. Yes, Joe was dead; they were trying to meet that fact squarely. But if they sold Journey's End it would be like severing the last tie with a man they adored.

Joe's illness had used up the family's savings, so Dave and Beth were trying to do all the work themselves, to make their four rooms in the ell livable. Dave found a few storm windows in the garage, and Beth washed them and he hung them. Mr. Richter brought a load of dry cornstalks and piled them around the ell's foundation, to cut down on the drafts. He also checked the old generator and found it was working, so the Harrisons would have some power in case the main line failed. However, the bitter cold of a northern winter was on its way.

They needed to concentrate on getting warm. Beth got an estimate from a local heating firm for insulating the ell and installing an oil furnace. She showed it to Dave because they were equal partners in any planning. All he could say was, "Wow!"

" 'Wow!' is right," she agreed. "If we went ahead we'd either have to put a new mortgage on the lodge or else we'd have to sell off some lake frontage."

"How about the money from the house in town, is that all gone?"

"Remember? We used it to pay off the last of the mortgage on this place."

Beth's hair was very short, brown curls with a bit of gray in them. When she was thinking hard she ran her hands through it so it stood on end, and it was standing on end now. "Let's try this on for size," she said. "Maybe, if we have some insulating done, we can get through the winter with only the wood stove. We could buy a couple of electric heaters, to take the chill off our bedrooms when it turns bitter cold.

"After school today, I dropped in to see the man who gave us that estimate. You know Ben Garcia, he was a good friend of your dad's. They were in Korea together, and when Joe was commander of the Veterans of Foreign Wars, Ben was vice commander. Ben told me that if we couldn't afford to hire his men to do the insulating, we could do some of the work ourselves. For instance, the fiber-glass batting or whatever they call it can be laid on the floor of the attic, between the floor joists. We could try to stuff loose fiber glass into the partitions. That would cut down on some of the drafts. To do the job right they'd blow the stuff loose into the walls with a machine, but that would cost a lot. Mr. Garcia also suggested that we weather-strip all the windows and doors.

"He asked about the stove. It worried him that we plan to heat with a wood stove, and he threatened to come out and inspect it, to make sure the chimney's safe. Or else he *promised;* I guess that was more like it. People are nice."

"Getting wood is no problem," Dave pointed

out. "That's a good deal we've got with Mr. Richter — that if we let him take his winter's firewood out of our woods, he'll cut ours. I figured he'd just cut it, and we'd have to haul it. But no, he saw me wrestling with a log, and he told me to leave it be. He said he'd haul our wood and stack it wherever you want it."

"Let's have him pile it right on the back porch, where it'll be handy," Beth suggested.

She looked around contentedly. The wind was blowing and the fire was roaring up the black pipe that led into the chimney. They were sitting at the table in their big, comfortable kitchen–living room. She had before her the inevitable pile of papers to correct, and Dave was putting together a plastic model of a Silver Shadow Rolls-Royce. Their eyes met, and he said what he knew she was thinking, "This isn't half bad; it's kind of cozy."

She nodded. "Here we are, you and I living the way they did a hundred years ago, and we're comfortable as two bugs in a rug. We won't be such a comfortable pair of bugs, though, when winter really hits!"

Dave set the half-finished model on the shelf over the sink and carefully gathered the remaining pieces into the box. "I'm out of glue," he said.

"Would you get another tube, the next time you shop?" She agreed.

He went to her, to kiss her good night. Maybe he was too old for that sort of thing, but he didn't know how to break the habit and didn't especially want to.

"I'll be up soon," she told him. "I want to write to Jim before I go to bed."

"Do you suppose we'll hear from him?" Dave asked.

"I don't expect so," she said. "I don't remember his ever writing us a letter."

Dave's room and hers were over the kitchen. Each had a hole cut in the floor, so the warmth from the stove would rise to take the chill off. The holes were covered with fancy metal grilles. Dave liked this arrangement; when his light was off and his room was dark he didn't feel alone.

The small bathroom had no such feature. It wouldn't freeze, during the long winter that lay ahead, because the pipes came up through the wall behind the stove; nevertheless it was a horrid, chilly place. Dave didn't waste any time admiring his homely, thin mug in the mirror; he washed and brushed his teeth in record time.

Back in his room he dug out a pair of flannel

23

pajamas from his bureau. Then he got down on his knees, to see if he could see his mother through the grille. Yes, she had poured herself a cup of coffee and was busy at the table correcting social studies papers. He was looking right down on the top of her head.

He thought, not for the first time or even the hundredth — maybe the thousandth — how lucky he was that when they handed out mothers he got such a classy, nervy, nice one.

Moonlight slanted across his bed, and before he got into it he went to the window. Tonight the moon was full, a great silver orb laying a wide shimmering path across the lake right to Dave's window.

Enoch's Pond it was called, for his great-great-grandfather, or even his great-great-great-grandfather — Dave was vague about family history. A pond it wasn't; it was truly a lake, deep, wide, two miles long, fringed with pine and hardwood forest.

Joe Harrison had loved it as though it were a living thing. Dave remembered how he had come home from his father's funeral and had stood looking at the lake, thinking how terribly, terribly wrong it was that a man had to die and leave behind people and a place he loved so much.

By now Dave knew all its moods. He thought he liked it best in summer, when the loons were flying, skimming the water, uttering the banshee cries that made your hair stand on end. Then he thought of winter, which would soon be upon them, when Enoch's Pond froze over and he would skate every day.

The Harrisons owned a good share of the shoreline on the west side. "No," Dave thought, "we must never, never sell an inch of it."

He got into bed, his eyes still full of that beautiful sight, the huge moon illuminating the dark water, the black pines, the feathery, naked forest.

He sniffed. His mother had re-heated the coffee and poured another cup. He thought of Jim. He'd really gotten a raw deal. That Nina, whom Dave had never seen, must be a nothing, a cipher, or even worse than a nothing, to cause such grief.

Dave's last thought was, "I wish I could send Jim a hunk of that scenery out there, the lake and the moon, so he'd have something nice to look at in the slammer."

3

THANKSGIVING was coming up, and Dave was well aware that his mother dreaded it as much as he did. She too was remembering last year.

That holiday had always been very big with Joe Harrison. He wanted a crowd around, so the Harrisons invited Mr. and Mrs. Richter and their two daughters, Emily and Louise. Then Joe did some investigating and found four old people in Hobb Creek who didn't expect to have any Thanksgiving.

The day came, and he helped with the work, laying a fire in the dining room of the lodge, setting the tables, stuffing two turkeys, fixing the vegetables. Then he drove to town and collected what he called his four "old folks."

The Richters brought cider and also some rare, wonderful German desserts. They ate in the lodge's main dining room, and the huge fire roared on the hearth, and it was a full, busy, happy day.

The thing Dave remembered most sharply about

that day, the memory that made his heart hurt, was his father's wide, happy grin and deep laughter. Jim was the son who had inherited Joe's sandy hair, his wide smile. Dave got his own dark, intense looks from his mother's side of the family.

What about Jim? Dave wondered. Would there by any holiday at that B.R.I., which whatever it was called was still a prison?

This Thanksgiving loomed up like a bleak prospect, a total washout. Then the Richters invited the Harrisons, and they went. They had to keep their spirits up; they couldn't spoil the day for others, and Dave guessed it was lucky this was so.

The Richters were a cheerful family. Their farmhouse was cheery and warm, and the food was out of this world. There was only one difficult incident. When the table was cleared, Mr. Richter got to his feet. "A toast to our good friend Joe," he said. "You don't have to stand, Beth — I know this is hard. But we must speak of Joe and I'll just say what's on my mind. Since it was God's will to take him, I'm glad he went quickly. Joe loved life and lived it fully, and if the cancer had dragged him down to being half a man he would have hated that. So let us be thankful we can drink to him, remembering only his wonderful laughter, and his kindness and goodness."

They drank in silence; there was nothing to say. Emily, the older girl, was sitting next to Dave. Her blue eyes were full of tears, and she put her arm around him and he hid his face in her cornsilk hair until the moment had passed.

Beth and Dave went home to the silent, empty lodge. Then something nice happened that took their minds off their troubles.

Beth poked up the fire in the kitchen range, and Dave stepped out on the back porch to fetch more stove wood. He happened to remember that he needed a clamp, to hold the car model he was working on. He was like his father and kept his tools neatly, so he opened the drawer of the work table knowing exactly where to put his hand on the clamp. Instead he put his hand on something furry.

He didn't yell; whatever the thing was, it didn't bite him. There was a flashlight in the drawer, and he snapped it on. In the corner of the drawer a half-grown opossum was curled in a circle, its coarse gray fur bristling.

Dave didn't touch it; he tapped gently on the under side of the drawer. The opossum huddled closer into itself but opened one eye. It didn't cry or squeak; it grumbled, like a human being whose sleep had been disturbed. Then the eye closed. Dave carefully shut the drawer.

He went inside. "Mom, you won't believe it, but a 'possum is sleeping in the tool drawer."

"Oh?" she said, not startled or fearful, because the Harrisons were used to living near wild things — near, but not quite this close. "Let's go see."

He showed her. "It wants to hibernate here," she said. "They're kind of cute, aren't they, when you don't see those awful bare snouts or the ratty tails?"

He tapped on the bottom of the drawer. This time the creature didn't open its eyes but it grumbled again. Beth had to laugh. "It sounds exactly like your grandfather when he wanted to sleep late in the morning and I had to wake him up."

"Shouldn't I take it out and let it loose in the woods?" Dave asked.

"It's here for its own good reasons," his mother said. "Maybe the rest of its family was killed. It knows better than we do what it needs."

"How about food?"

"It got in by itself, so it can go out by itself, to look for food. But just in case it might like a snack, we'll fix it a sandwich."

He thought she meant peanut butter, because

they threw out peanut butter sandwiches for an old fox that sometimes came mooching around. Instead, she spread the bread with bacon fat, and when Dave asked why, she reminded him that was what Joe had fed a sick opossum which he had nursed back to health. Dave put the sandwich in the drawer, saying, "Here's your supper, fella," but the animal was sleeping soundly. In fact it was breathing so slowly its fur scarcely moved.

They put in more wood and turned the dampers to cut down the draft. Dave suggested it was time to shut up shop and go to bed. "I suppose so," his mother said, but she sounded reluctant. Her nights were probably very lonely; sometimes in the night Dave saw the dim glow of the light in her room, where she was reading to pass the hours.

"Dave, there's no school tomorrow," she went on. "I wonder if you'll go with me to the Richters in the pickup. Feeding that 'possum reminded me, the heavy snows are coming and the deer will be hungry. Mr. Richter will spare us a few bales of hay, because he put down two good crops last summer."

"Okay, Mom."

Dave was at the door when she spoke again. "Dave," she said, "Mr. Richter was right about your dad. It startled me when he spoke out like that at dinner, but he saw the truth, that your father would have hated being a helpless invalid. At first I would have been terribly hurt if anyone said such a thing, but enough time has gone by so I can see, Mr. Richter was right."

"I guess so," Dave said. He waited, but she didn't go on, so he went up to bed.

In October, when the leaves went, when he and his mother faced the winter, Dave had wondered whether life at Journey's End wouldn't be dull and boring. It didn't turn out that way. Shortly after November turned the corner into December, snow came, six inches of it.

The woods seemed to move closer to the lodge. Dave found he was listening harder. One night he heard a faint crackling in the woods. His window was open only a few inches, but the silence was so profound the slightest sound came in.

He kept a flashlight in his bed table. He crept to the window, raised it higher, and luckily it didn't squeak. He snapped on the light, directing the strong beam into the woods.

What he saw was eyes. They were on different levels, some higher, some lower, and he counted ten pairs.

He didn't snap off the light because he knew deer were mesmerized by light, and if it went out they would wheel and vanish. He left it on the windowsill and stole into his mother's room. "Mom, come and look," he whispered.

She came silently and knelt at the windowsill with him. "Oh," she whispered, "isn't that lovely — they've found the hay. Dave, there's a stag, and five does, and four young ones. I just hope they're old enough to survive when the cold gets bitter. We'll have to keep putting out more hay as the snow deepens. Turn off the light now, son, and let them go."

He did so and heard the crackle of twigs breaking. When he snapped it back on seconds later, the glowing eyes had vanished.

He asked Beth the next day when the hunting season ended. She didn't know but thought it would be over soon. All the land around Enoch's Pond was posted against hunting, so the area wasn't often bothered by what the local people called "the slobs," the city men who came with their beautiful rifles and wearing their red check shirts and silly red caps. Just the same, Dave was concerned. He felt kind of rich, knowing the Harrisons had a real herd of deer, and couldn't bear the thought of some slob coming and decimating the herd.

Joe Harrison had owned a revolver, a .38 Smith and Wesson; and Dave got it out one night to clean it, taking a long time with the job because it was a pleasure, putting such a fine instrument into good condition. His mother must have noticed his pleasure because she said, "I didn't think you were fond of guns."

"I wouldn't kill, any more than Dad would kill," Dave said defensively.

"No, I know you wouldn't," she said quickly. "I think it's fine that your Dad taught you to shoot at targets, and how to handle guns properly. But you're just like your Dad. You couldn't possibly kill, just for the pleasure of killing."

"It's just that we shouldn't allow it to rust."

"Quite right," she agreed.

These days they talked about guns, they talked about school, they talked about what they wanted for supper, but they didn't talk about Christmas. That holiday hung over them, like a nightmare in the background. The holiday season had started, and Hobb Creek's Main Street was decorated and the stores were bright with Christmas merchandise.

Out of his allowance Dave had saved enough to buy his mother a nice sweater, and doubtless she was buying him presents. But what kind of a holiday could they possibly have? Oh, the Richters would probably invite them again for dinner, and they might even put up a tree in the kitchen. But the way it looked to Dave, it would be a real drag, something to be endured. He longed for January, when the season of joy and merriment would be behind them.

His mother's mind worked along parallel lines, and she said one evening, "This time of year, it makes it harder that we don't have any relatives. I mean, your dad was an only child, and I was an only child, and all your grandparents are gone now."

Dave brought the name out as though he was laying it on the table before them. "But I'm not an only child. There's Jim."

"You've been thinking about him too," she said. "Dave, right after that horrible occasion last fall, did you have any conversation with anyone here locally about it?"

"I guess people knew," Dave told her. "They saw the piece in the paper and put two and two together. I didn't think fast enough to lie about it, at school. Why, Mom?"

"It's just as well you didn't deny it was our Jim. I suppose it was all over Hobb Creek. The principal at the high school asked me and I didn't make any bones about it. I said yes, he was Joe's son by his former marriage. What I'm getting at now, though, is that if you think about Jim, and I think about him, we ought to talk about him. Maybe we ought to *do* something about him. I mean, we're lonely, but

34

we're together. But he's lonely all alone in that institution."

"Did you have something in mind?"

"I'd like to go to see him, and take him gifts."

"All right."

"You wouldn't just prefer to try to forget all
about him?"

"No," Dave said briefly, because he didn't want
to talk about it anymore. He didn't know how he felt
about Jim. Sometimes he just wanted to forget he
had a half brother. Then there were times when he
really did feel fond of Jim, because he remembered
the time five years ago when Jim had visited and the
two had felt very close.

Dave pushed this problem away. He put the revolver in the kitchen drawer where it was always
kept, got out his books, and made believe he was
studying.

After that, oddly, things began to look up for the
Harrisons, as far as Christmas was concerned.
Maybe it wasn't such a big deal, buying gifts and
planning a visit to Jim, but it gave Dave and his
mother a sense of sharing in the spirit of Christmas.
Which Dave secretly suspected wasn't as joyous for a
lot of people as they made it out to be.

Now that they were planning for Jim, Dave and

Beth went on to plan for Joe Harrison's "old folks." There were only three now, one woman having died. Beth suggested they fix a real Christmas dinner and invite Mr. Stommer who lived alone over his cobbler shop, Mrs. Brown whose relatives couldn't stand her, and Miss Samantha Flint who was in her seventies, an irascible bag of ancient bones who had taught Latin all her life in the high school until she was retired. Dave grumbled to his mother, "It looks like we're getting all the losers," but just the same he was very glad she suggested it.

It was easy to assemble the gifts for their old folks. Putting together a collection for Jim was harder. They had no idea what a person who lived in a prison cell wanted or needed. They ended up by buying a box of candy, a lot of chewing gum, a bottle of shaving cologne, two pairs of wool socks because Dave thought it might be cold there, and some paperback books.

They didn't know that Jim liked to read. But Beth, being a teacher, figured that people ought to have books around.

They wrapped these gifts in gay papers and ribbons and packed them in a shopping bag. Beth had called long distance and learned that Jim was allowed visitors once a month, and this date came on a Tuesday, ten days before Christmas. She didn't inquire whether fourteen-year-old brothers could be counted as visitors, and suspected the prison authorities might not let Dave in. "We'll take our chances and try to bluff them into letting you see Jim," she said.

She got a substitute teacher for a day, and on that bright, crisp Tuesday morning she and Dave set out on the long drive to Burrows.

4

THEY ARRIVED in Burrows an hour before visiting hours began, so they found a Howard Johnson's and had lunch. Beth was fidgety and finally she admitted, "I'm scared."

Dave was too but he asked, "Scared of what?"

"I don't know," she said. "I suppose because this is a new situation. Your dad had a theory that people ought to welcome new situations, but I don't believe that included going to see a relative in prison."

When they were back in the car Beth stopped at a gas station, had the tank filled, and asked directions. The attendant didn't appear surprised that a respectable-looking woman was visiting somebody at B.R.I. He only said, "Keep on this road, ma'am, and watch for gates on the right. There's a sign."

The gates were open, and a guard stepped out as they drove through, but he waved them on. They followed a long, landscaped drive, and Dave said, relieved, "This doesn't look too awful." When they came to the top of the hill, though, there was the Institute ahead, and it did look awful, like a prison on TV, brick buildings surrounded by a high wire fence.

A guard at this gate stopped them to ask whom they wanted to see. He took down their names, and asked how old Dave was. "It's all right," he said. "At Christmas time we relax the rules. Youngsters over twelve are allowed, if they're visiting a relative. You want to see your brother, sonny?"

This gave Dave something to think about, while his mother parked the car and they walked to the entrance. Jim was no blood relation of Beth's and she didn't have to be here. But here she was, determined to be kind to Jim, another woman's son. Dave felt a twinge of resentment; he wasn't at all sure he wanted to share his mother with anybody. Then he resolutely put that down. He couldn't be jealous of Jim.

They got into a hassle as soon as they passed through the main door. They were directed to a counter, and the guard behind the counter ordered Dave to set the shopping bag on it and then stand back. He laid the gifts out and began slitting the wrappers. "Do you have to do that?" Beth protested. "We tried to wrap them nicely!"

"Ma'am, I have to. I'll be careful, and you can wrap them up again when I'm through."

"What are you looking for?" Beth asked.

"Drugs, guns, knives, explosives, nail files, shoehorns, you name it, we're looking for it."

"Do we look like the kind who would try to smuggle explosives into a prison?" Beth asked, smiling to butter him up.

"The ones who do it never look like the kind," he said.

He riffled through the pages of the paperback books, felt inside the wool socks, opened the package of shaving lotion and examined it. He set aside the chewing gum and candy. "Your son will get those after we've looked at them more carefully," he explained.

Another family was waiting to have their gifts examined, so the Harrisons moved outside. They rewrapped the packages as best they could, but it had become an untidy little collection. "I felt awful before, but I feel worse now," Beth muttered as they went down the hall.

Dave expected they'd only see Jim through a glass wall or a wire enclosure, but no, the reception room had chairs and tables, and Jim was sitting at a table watching the door. His pale hair was clipped short and his wide face was full of joy. "Hey, I've got company!" he shouted, and grabbed Beth around the waist.

40

A guard quickly stepped up. "None of that, Jim. I warned you, you're not supposed to touch your visitors," he said, and Jim let Beth go.

They sat at the table. "Why can't you touch us?" Dave asked.

"This is a suspicious bunch," Jim said. "They figured you'd pass me some contraband. Beth, you look beautiful!"

"Come off it, Jim, I never in my life looked beautiful," she protested.

"You do too look beautiful. I never thought you'd come. You drove all this way to see me." To Dave's amazement, Jim's eyes filled with tears.

"How's it going?" Dave asked, his voice coming out as a croak because he was so nervous.

Jim got hold of himself. "It's okay, Davey. They're not too strict if you go by the book. Some of the guys are great. I've got a good job, I work with the outside crew, shoveling snow, stuff like that. If I'm here next spring I'll help cut the grass and take care of the flowers. So I'm not shut in all day. I've got a pal, Cuffy, and I've got a friend, Mr. Maxwell, who's the social worker. I asked him to come here to meet you. I mean, I wanted him to know I've got a real family."

Jim anxiously watched the clock, because visits were limited to a half hour. He asked about the lodge. He had really adored that place. He inquired about Herman, then said he'd known Herman five years ago, so he supposed that raccoon was long gone. Dave told him about the herd of deer which was staying close to Journey's End because Dave was putting out hay for them, and described the opossum which was hibernating in the tool drawer. "I wish I could see that 'possum," Jim said wistfully.

A guard came over and put his hand on Jim's shoulder and said, "Time's up, lad."

A young man in a business suit was standing nearby. "Here's Mr. Maxwell," Jim said, and introduced them. He thanked Beth again for the gifts and told her he'd probably receive the candy and chewing gum okay. The guard wouldn't confiscate them because this was an honest place. "For a slammer, it's not too bad," he said, grinning at the guard. Then he astonished them all by gently taking Beth's hand and kissing it. He seized Dave's and squeezed it so hard Dave had to yell. "Sorry, little brother!" Jim exclaimed, and rushed to the door. A guard unlocked it and he vanished.

They watched him go. "He's a nice boy," Beth said.

"Yes, he is," Mr. Maxwell agreed, "but he's not an easy one to understand. Please sit down, Mrs.

Harrison. I'd like to talk with you and Dave for a few minutes."

His first question shook Dave. "In your opinion, Mrs. Harrison, is Jim disturbed? Is he dangerous?"

Beth too seemed jarred by the question. "I have no idea," she stammered. "I'm not his real mother, you know. His father and I talked about it a little. Jim visited us, and most of the time he seemed like a normal, healthy boy. And yet, we knew he must have emotional scars, because of the kind of life he was living. I suppose his actions prove that. His father couldn't get custody of him, so there wasn't much we could do for Jim."

"We've tried to locate his real mother," Mr. Maxwell said. "She has left New Orleans and has disappeared.

"We want to do a good rehabilitation job here," he went on. "When a boy's time is up, we don't like to turn him loose with no place to go. Too often they run afoul of the law and come right back. I haven't talked with Jim about this, but when he told me you were coming today I decided to ask you. Jim's time will be up soon. Is there any chance he could come to you for a while? So he could get his life started again in a good direction?"

The question was so unexpected Beth didn't answer. Dave was shocked too, and his face was probably blank as she asked, "What do you think, Dave?"

"I don't know," he mumbled.

"You teach in the local high school, Mrs. Harrison. Oh, I've made a few inquiries. You have a place in the community, and I can understand that Jim's staying with you would disrupt your lives and might be very difficult. But frankly, I don't have any alternative except to ask you, because otherwise we can't release Jim when his time is up. We'd assume he'd find bad companions. The boy is easily led, and I'm afraid he'd be back here in no time at all. Or worse, it would be the State prison next time. And that, I'm afraid, would be the end of him."

The social worker stopped, waited. "Think it over, Mrs. Harrison," he suggested, when Beth didn't speak. "I'll call you after the holidays. If you decide against it, I'll understand. I can imagine that your life is not an easy one, and such a complication would make it more difficult."

'We'll think about it," Beth said. "All right, Dave?"

"Yeah, sure," Dave agreed.

The Harrisons did little talking on the long drive home. Dave was confused. When he first saw Jim in the visiting room, when Jim grabbed his hand and wrung it, Dave's heart had lifted. Jim was the only brother he would ever have. Jim had looked different, with his bristly crew cut, but he was the same Jim Dave remembered, warm and enthusiastic.

Later on, when the social worker had asked about Jim coming to live in Hobb Creek, Dave's heart had sunk. Maybe he was being purely selfish, but he didn't want to share his home and his mother and his life with Jim. Was he ashamed because Jim was in trouble with the law? Maybe he was, and he couldn't help that, either.

Another thought hit him that really shook him. Was he jealous of Jim because Jim looked so exactly like Joe Harrison, broad, tall, wide-faced, with a grin exactly like their father's?

Dave glanced at his mother. She seemed withdrawn, intent only on her driving. Finally he began, "Mom, about Jim."

"Let's think about it for a while," was all she said.

They had other things to cope with, in the short time before Christmas. The weather gave them a hard time. A lot of snow fell.

The macadam road which circled the lake was a school bus route and also a milk route, so the town plowed it promptly after a storm. However, the lane from the lodge out to the road was eight hundred feet long. Mr. Richter plowed it for the Harrisons, but he couldn't always get there at seven in the morning, when Beth had to leave. The morning after the December fall it was touch and go whether she'd make it out the lane.

Usually Dave left the house before she did and walked to the road to meet his bus, but today he stayed to help her. A dozen times he had to shovel around the wheels and put down a heavy mat for traction. Studded tires weren't much help in six inches of light snow.

Heat was another big concern. After the storm the thermometer hovered around zero, the wind whistled, and the Harrisons were just plain freezing to death. Beth asked Ben Garcia to come and assess the situation.

He paid a visit and studied it. The ell had a peaked roof, and under it a windowless attic which was reached by folding stairs and a trap door in the upstairs hall. Mr. Garcia tapped the attic floor, tapped all the walls, and decided that a satisfactory job could be done without a professional team. 'I'll do it myself, with Dave for a helper," he announced.

Beth sensed he intended to do the job for free, because of his friendship with Joe Harrison. "You can't set foot on the place if you don't let me pay you, Ben," she said.

"Hah!" he said. "You're a competent woman and independent as a pig on ice, as I can see, but you're not very big. If you try to interfere I'll pick you up and put you to one side, out of Dave's and my way. You'll pay for the materials, and that's all!"

He checked the wood stove and the chimney to make sure they were safe, and promised he would be back on his first free day.

The weather cooperated during Christmas week; it turned warm and the lane dried out. School ended the Wednesday before the holiday. They set up a small tree in the corner of the kitchen. It was out of the question to hold the party in the lodge dining room; it was cold as Greenland's icy mountains in there.

On Christmas Eve all was ready, the gifts were wrapped and under the tree, the turkey was stuffed, most of the cooking was done. Dave went outside to fetch enough wood to carry them through the next day.

He stood listening to the wonderful stillness of the forest. The deer were probably out there, and the raccoons, the foxes, the skunks, the opossums, the porcupines, the little animals, mice and voles and moles — they were probably listening to him. He had a good relation with all these unseen creatures. They trusted him although their lives didn't often touch, unless one came in from the cold, like the opossum. Dave was thinking that the next day the opossum ought to get an extra slather of bacon fat on its bread.

A long, high, hopeless wail cut the silence, from the direction of the lake, and Dave stiffened. He hoped in his heart he wouldn't hear it again, but he did. That meant he would have to do something about it.

He fumbled in the tool drawer for the flashlight, and the opossum grumbled sleepily. He said nothing to his mother, but set out. The night was moonless, but the stars blazed brightly. Dave knew the area like the back of his hand, and there was nothing to fear. Unless, of course, he stumbled into a bear. But bears were scarce, and they were hibernating now.

The wail came again, guiding him, some animal in terrible distress. He crossed the lawn that slanted down to the lake, toward the stand of tall pines near the end of the Harrison land. The cry rang out, inland, a dozen yards away. He stumbled over a rock he'd forgotten, and righted himself. Whatever it was, the creature was under the pines.

Pine needles carpeted the ground. There it was, a cat thrashing on the ground, and it shrieked at sight of him. He saw that its forepaw was held fast in a trap, and he caught the dark gleam of blood. He bent over the cat, murmuring, but it was out of its mind with pain, and slashed at his face with its free paw.

He needed a crowbar and he needed help. He ran home and burst through the kitchen door. "Ma, there's a cat in a trap, so come on!"

She got her coat immediately, obeying, but she said, "Wait, Dave, let's think what we need before we go."

"We just need the short bar."

"And a blanket, because the cat will fight us."

They set out, Dave leading because he knew the land better than she did. He had to wait once for her to catch up, and she said, "Dave, who would set a trap on our land?"

"I don't know, but I'm going to find out," he said.

He led her to the spot. She knelt on the dry pine needles, exclaiming, "Whoever did it, I could strangle him with my bare hands!"

5

BETH FOLDED the thin blanket around the screaming cat so only the caught paw was exposed, then directed the flash beam for Dave. He was so full of rage his hands shook, and she said, "Get hold of yourself, son, if you want to help the poor thing."

He fought for control, and his hands steadied. He got the end of the bar into the teeth of the trap and parted them long enough for his mother to pull the cat loose. It was fighting and howling inside the blanket, not knowing friend from foe. Beth got its head free and cradled it in her arms, murmuring, "Puss, puss, puss." The cat quieted down, but it was still shuddering and crying.

Dave helped his mother to her feet. Then he felt around under the needles and found the wires that held the trap in place. He jerked the whole thing loose, and he ran to the shore of the lake and threw it as far as he could, hearing the splash as it crashed through the skim of ice.

They set out for home, Beth carrying the cat, Dave guiding her by the elbow. "Somebody must have laid a line," he said. "I'll find every one of the damned traps and get rid of them."

"The Websters own the next land," his mother reminded him. "They're only here summers, their home is in Boston. Maybe they gave someone permission to trap their land."

"You could call them and ask," Dave suggested. Then he changed his mind. "No, don't call. Because whether they gave permission or not I'm going to pull the traps."

She didn't argue. Her silence meant it was up to him to do what he thought was right, Dave realized with pride.

Home in their kitchen, they opened the blanket and looked at their prize. Maybe once it had been a handsome, long-haired tiger; but now its fur was matted and dirty and its ribs stuck out. Dave held it while Beth fixed an antiseptic solution and brought clean rags. The cat howled and thrashed while she gently tested to see if bones were broken. None were, but the flesh was badly torn. By the time Beth finished bathing the wound Dave was nauseated, sick as a dog. He thought she ought to bandage the leg but she said no, the cat could take care of it better than they could.

They fixed a box for a bed and set out a dish of milk and another of crumbled meatloaf. Then Beth said, "Let's leave it alone and go up to bed."

The last thing, Dave bent to pet it. It was attacking the food as though it had been starved for many days. He felt the fur quiver in its neck, and stooped down to listen. The cat was purring. "What'll we do with it, after it's well?" he asked. "Can we keep it?"

"Of course," his mother said. "We know it doesn't belong to the Richters, so it must be an abandoned cat."

"You said we couldn't have a dog because it would be a danger to the wild animals. So how can we keep a cat?"

"It'll have to learn," his mother said. "It's live-and-let-live, around here, and the cat will have to be taught that lesson."

"What do you want to call it?"

She was ready with an answer. "How about 'Mose'? Your dad used to tell about a wonderful cat named Mose he owned when he was a boy, and that was a male tiger too."

Before he went to bed Dave got down on his knees to look through the hole in his floor. Mose was curled in his box, carefully licking the wounded paw.

He looked much better next morning; sometime

during the night he had given himself a thorough bath. When Dave clattered down the stairs Mose came to meet him, hopping on three legs. Dave fixed him a bowl of bread and milk and Mose finished it off fast, as though he was afraid food was going out of style.

It was only six o'clock. This was Christmas morning, and a big day lay ahead, with gifts, and then chores, and the dinner party at noon; but Dave had one job he had to get out of the way first. The morning was clear and cold. He put on two wool shirts, heavy gloves, and a wool cap and set out, armed with the crowbar.

He found the first trap just over the line where a cairn of stones marked the Websters' property. He was hoping and praying he wouldn't find any animals, either dead or alive, caught in the vicious leghold traps, and his luck was in. He thought, "The better the day the better the deed." Maybe it was because this was Christmas morning that the job went so easily. He located four more traps on the Websters' land and threw them into the lake where they sank forever.

Whoever had laid them was an amateur who didn't know enough to conceal them. Was it some kid from town, some kid he knew at school? The next time he went to Hobb Creek he would inquire at the hardware store whether any-local person had bought them. The things cost around ten dollars apiece, so some slob was out sixty dollars.

He must have looked pleased with himself because his mother looked up from the stove where she was cooking breakfast and said, "You found them. I thought you would. Merry Christmas! What did you do with them?"

"I threw them in the lake."

"Oh," she said. "Maybe you should have kept them. We may be in a wee bit of trouble because you destroyed property."

"I think what I did was right," Dave said stubbornly.

She gave him a long look. "Maybe so," she agreed.

The rest of the day went well. Beth liked her sweater, and Dave was delighted with a new pair of showshoes. His big surprise was a bicycle. It came in a big box and had to be assembled, but that was no chore — that would be fun. Now he had a fine new set of wheels; his bike had given up the ghost last fall, bent and crippled like a spavined old horse.

He looked after the cooking while his mother went to town to collect the guests. She ushered them into the kitchen as though she was shooing a flock of hens, and took their coats and seated them around the stove. Another round of gift exchanging followed, and Beth received a beautiful handmade quilt from Mrs. Brown. Mr. Stommer gave Dave a ship model he had made from a kit, and Miss Samantha Flint presented him with a dictionary and told him that if he learned every word in it then he could call himself educated. "I did a good job of teaching your daddy and I only wish I wasn't retired so I could go to work on you, David," she said severely.

The three liked all their little gifts. It was a gay crowd that sat down to the elegant meal. Even Mose got a great dinner. He seemed dazed by the sudden change in his fortunes. "He went awful fast from rags to riches," Mrs. Brown commented.

Mrs. Richter had told Beth not to make any desserts, and the Richter family arrived loaded down with pies, cake, pudding, and a gallon of hard cider. For a couple of hours the crowded kitchen was the scene of such gaiety, there was no room for sad thoughts.

Later, Mr. Richter offered to drive the guests back to town. The leave-taking was tender; they were shaky and grateful, and all gently kissed Beth and Dave good-bye.

They did the dishes and tidied the kitchen. Dave decided to put off until the next day the pleasure of assembling his new bicycle. Beth was tired, and went to her room early, but not before she had looked around the warm room with its twinkling tree and said contentedly, "It was a good old Christmas after all, wasn't it, son?" He agreed with that.

He was just dropping off to sleep when he heard muffled sounds, and knew she was crying. He sat up, wanting to go to her, then changed his mind. He couldn't say, "Don't do that because Dad wouldn't like it." No, she had a right to cry. He felt like crying, himself. Sometimes, like tonight, he missed his father so much, he could hardly bear it, and the load of responsibility which had been dumped on him seemed like more than he could endure.

During Christmas week the thermometer dropped sharply and the lake froze over again. The Harrisons were hard put to it to keep even tolerably warm. Ben Garcia called. "Bitter cold, ain't it, boy?" he said, when Dave answered the phone. "Is your ma there?"

"No, she's in town, shopping."

"I'll make do with you, then. I'm coming tomorrow with a truckload of stuff, to see what I can do about making your place cozier. I'll need your help all day. You'll be there, boy?"

"I'll be here," Dave assured him.

Lew Collins came back with Beth; he had been invited to spend a couple of days at Journey's End because the skating was so great. He thought insulating the place sounded like fun, and Dave didn't argue, but it crossed Dave's mind that Lew had a weird idea of fun.

Dave was right. Mr. Garcia showed up at nine the next morning, and he ran the boys ragged, hauling huge cartons of insulating stuff up the narrow folding stairs to the attic. The floor boards of the attic weren't nailed down but were laid loose. Dave and Lew waited on Mr. Garcia hand and foot while he tore the thick battens of fiber glass into the proper lengths and laid them between the floor joists.

That was the easy part of the job; the other part was horrible. The only way to get at the interior and exterior walls was by dropping loose fiber glass down the partitions. It was frigid, up there in the attic, and the stuff the three worked with was shredded and fine, getting in their mouths and eyes and up their noses.

Lew was a good sport and didn't complain. Finally Dave said to him, "I bet the next time you come to visit, you'll find out first what kind of a project we've got in mind."

"That's the truth, you can depend on it!" Lew agreed.

Mr. Garcia didn't allow much time for idle conversation, but hustled the boys along, snapping orders. They pushed as much of the fiber glass as possible into the partitions. Finally Mr. Garcia pronounced the job finished, and the boys dragged the empty cartons down the stairs and outside.

They came right back in and Dave started to pull a chair up to the stove but Mr. Garcia yelled, "You'll get that stuff all over your ma's clean room!" He marched the boys outdoors again and the three shook themselves and slapped each other over thoroughly, to get rid of the feathery, clinging insulating material. Mr. Garcia made the boys shake out their hair. "There's some advantage in being bald like me," he observed. Only when they were clean would he go inside, where Beth had a hot meal waiting for them.

As soon as they had eaten Mr. Garcia got up to leave. They tried to thank him, but he edged out the door. "It's little enough to do for Joe!" he called back.

The difference was startling. "Oh boy," Dave said, "this is really living!" The rooms were so warm, Mose left his box by the stove and limped upstairs to join the boys. Lew had brought his sleeping bag, and slept on Dave's floor.

The next day Beth wouldn't allow the boys to do any work. The skating on Enoch's Pond was perfect. Anybody was welcome to skate there, and other kids from town came. They built a fire on shore and toasted marshmallows and it was a great day.

Once, while they were resting, Lew mentioned to Dave, "Bert Warden laid a trapline out here somewhere, do you know about it? When he came out to walk his line he found the traps were gone."

"Huh," was all Dave said, but his heart banged. So the traps belonged to Bert Warden. Of all the boys in town, why did they have to belong to him? Bert was a natural leader because he was big, and smart. His father was an officer of the bank, so the Wardens were important citizens. Dave and Bert had never hit it off, and all hell would break loose when Bert found out who had pulled his traps.

Dave didn't mention to Lew that the traps lay under the lake's thick ice. He thought to himself, "Why do I always back away from trouble with Bert? Someday I'm going to have to stand up to him, and it might as well be sooner as later."

The old year had drawn to a close. On the last day the Harrisons had a telephone call that changed their quiet life. Beth answered, and listened, and said, "I'll have to talk to my son."

She covered the receiver with her hand. "Dave, it's Mr. Maxwell, the man we met at Burrows. He says Jim can be released in January if we're willing to take him in. I wish we'd talked this over. What do you think?"

Dave didn't know what he thought because the question had come at him too suddenly. "Whatever you want to do, Mom," he said.

"If we don't, he'll be kept there until spring, and then turned loose to fend for himself."

She waited, but Dave didn't speak, and she said, "I'd like to give it a try. I'd like to say yes."

What else could Dave say? "Okay, tell him Jim can come."

"Mr. Maxwell, it's all right," she told the man on the phone. "You'll bring him over? Just let us know a day ahead."

After this call, although now they knew Jim was coming, they still didn't talk about it much. They cleared out the storage room off the kitchen, and borrowed furniture from the lodge to fix it up as a bedroom, the way it had been when Jim had stayed at Journey's End five years ago.

Dave knew Beth was puzzled by his attitude, but he couldn't help it. "We don't really know him," Dave thought. "We don't know what his life was like in those years when we never saw him or heard from him. All we know is that he's big and good-looking and he's Dad's son."

It was hard enough getting through the winter days, going to school, helping his mother with her car in the morning, doing the chores, keeping enough wood in the house. Dave thought, "What we don't need is more complications."

On a Friday in mid-January Mr. Maxwell called to say that he was bringing Jim the next day.

That Saturday morning Beth gave Jim's room a good cleaning and then cooked things she knew Jim liked. Now that the change was upon them she seemed pleased about it. Dave couldn't help feeling somewhat sour. He was there all the time, working hard, doing his job. The big welcome, though, was being laid on for Jim, who was like that character in the Bible, the Prodigal Son.

In early afternoon a black state car with the B.R.I. insignia on the door came up the lane. The minute it was parked Jim shot out and rushed to the door where they waited, shouting, "Ma, Ma, I made it! I'm here!"

Badly jolted, Dave stood by and watched. Jim's face was rosy from the cold. He looked so much like his father, for a second Dave hated him. Luckily Dave had control of his own face and none of this showed. Jim seized him and held him close and said in a low voice, "Little brother, thanks for letting me come."

6

THE DAY of Jim's arrival went okay, although Dave didn't sleep too well that night; he was too conscious of another human being in the house.

On Sunday morning he came downstairs early. He had assembled his new bike according to the manual that came with it, but he was having trouble getting the chain adjusted. He hauled it into the kitchen and was working on it when Jim appeared. "I thought you'd sleep late," Dave commented.

"At B.R.I. they don't let you snooze in the morning," Jim told him. He came over to look. "I'll help you," he said.

"Are you good with things like this?"

"Boy, am I! But first I want to go outside."

Dave could see him through the window. The minute Jim shut the door he was off and running. His speed startled Dave, and Dave thought, "Maybe he's going to run right out of our lives again."

Dave didn't know what to do. Should he wake up his mother so she could chase after Jim in the car? He watched at the window, getting very nervous. Then he saw Jim reappear at the end of the lane. Jim came up the road full speed and flung open the door. "Boy, that was great!" he exclaimed. "That's what gets to you when you're in the can. You can never stretch your legs."

"I was scared," Dave said frankly. "I thought you'd really taken off."

"Took off for where?"

"I don't know. The wild blue yonder?"

"Why would I want to do a thing like that? Just when I've got it made?" Jim sounded amazed.

"How about some coffee?" Dave asked, and started to fill the teakettle.

"No," Jim said. "A little squirt like you needs cocoa, that's full of good stuff. I'll make it."

He did, and it was good, and they made a lot of toast and ate almost half a loaf of bread. Then Jim went to work on the bike. There seemed to be some magic in his fingers; the chain went on perfectly for him. When Beth came down the boys were laughing and kidding, and she looked happy to see them together like that.

Over that weekend Jim worked every moment. He seemed to think he had to prove himself. He fixed Beth's washing machine, he scrubbed the kitchen floor, he cut kindling and hauled an enormous amount of wood, doubling the size of Dave's woodpile. It seemed to Dave he was working terribly hard at the job of getting himself liked.

Monday morning came, and by then Jim was firmly set as a member in good standing. He saw Beth and Dave off to school, assuring them he would take care of the place. Mose was on his shoulder, and he waved Mose's paw in a playful good-bye.

Dave looked back morosely. It was okay for Jim to act like the lord of the manor, maybe. He, Dave, had to meet the world, and the way news traveled in a town like Hobb Creek, the story would be all around school that his criminal brother was living at Journey's End.

He was right. Lew Collins was anxiously waiting for Dave's bus. "Louise Richter says your brother's living at your house," Lew began. "She says they saw him running on the road."

"That's right," Dave said. "Jim's going to be with us for a while until he gets straightened out."

"If Bert Warden knows, I bet he'll say something. He's looking for a chance to make trouble. He claims you're the one who stole his traps."

"I'm not scared of Bert Warden," Dave said, straightening his spine and sounding tough.

"If you're not, you ought to be," Lew said. "He's twice your size."

Maybe Lew was small, smaller than Dave, but he was a good friend, and he made sure he was at Dave's side when Bert accosted him. They were all in the hot-lunch line, shuffling along with their trays. Bert left his place in the line and came over. "I hear your jailbird brother's in town," he said. "It looks like everybody had better buy new locks because he'll probably lift anything that isn't nailed down. But that runs in your family, doesn't it?"

Dave stared into Bert's angry face and lost his nerve. "I don't know what you're talking about," he stammered.

"You know what I mean. You stole six traps off me, and they cost ten dollars apiece. If you're smart you'll hand them over right now. I had permission from the Websters to lay that trap line."

"You sure didn't have permission to set one on our land!"

"I never set a trap on your land!"

"Oh yes, you did." Dave squared off. He had his nerve back now.

The women who served the hot lunch were listening and looked upset. Mrs. Willower, the principal, came over and ordered, "All right, boys, that's enough."

"You bring those traps to school with you tomorrow morning," Bert ordered in a low voice.

Lew and Dave carried their trays to a table. "Did you really pull his traps?" Lew asked.

"Yes. You know that cat, Mose, we've got at our house? He was caught in one. Those leghold traps are a real lousy deal."

"Are you going to give them back?"

"I can't," Dave said. "I threw them in the lake."

"You did? That's great!"

"That's easy for you to say," Dave told Lew. "You don't have to face Bert tomorrow. But I guess he can't do any worse than kill me."

That afternoon Dave told his mother about it. "Mom, I'm in a jam," he said. "You know those traps? It turns out they belonged to Bert Warden, and he wants them back, but I can't give them back because where I threw them the lake's twenty, thirty feet deep."

"Oh my Lord, Davey," she said. "Bert Warden is that big bully in your room. He must be twice your size."

"He isn't really a bully. But he's awfully mad. What do you think I ought to do tomorrow?"

Dave really expected her to say, "We'll have to buy him new traps." She said no such thing. "It serves him right and I'm glad you threw them in the lake," she told Dave. "I'm quite sure the Websters never gave him permission. If you can take what you'll have to take from Bert, at school, then I'll back you up a hundred percent if his father tries to make trouble. But we won't replace those wicked things just so he can set them somewhere else!"

Jim had heard enough of this discussion to join in. "If this Warden guy is so big, you'd better let me take care of him."

"No," Dave said. "Thanks just the same, Jim, but I have to fight my own wars."

"Not when the other guy is twice your size."

"There isn't going to be any war," Beth said. "I think I'd better take the matter up with Bert's father."

Dave was near crying, he felt so frustrated. "Ma, you can't fight my wars either! I won't let you!"

"What if this guy really beats up on you?" Jim asked.

"If he does, he does," Dave said.

They ate dinner — not that Dave ate much. Dusk had settled down, but just the same he put on his heavy jacket and cap and started out. Jim said, "I'll come with you," but Dave said, "No." He had to think things out for himself.

He walked along the shoreline, kicking at loose stones, thinking. He came up with one conclusion.

Maybe the key to the whole mess was whether the Websters had or had not given Bert permission to trap their land.

He ran back home. Beth was finishing the dishes, and she looked relieved when he reappeared. "Mom, I've got to find out for sure whether Mr. Webster gave Bert permission," Dave said. "I want to call him."

"Go ahead," Beth said. "Mr. Richter looks after their place during the winter, so he'll have their Boston number. Do you want me to talk to Mr. Webster?"

"No." Dave's conviction was growing, these days, that the time had come for him to start standing on his own feet. He couldn't tag along forever, doing what his mother thought best, and in the meantime waiting for fate to clobber him. Fate being Bert Warden.

"Do you want me to get the number for you?"

"No, I'll do it."

He telephoned and explained the situation to Mr. Richter. Then he didn't ask his mother how to dial out of state, but figured it out from the directions in the telephone book.

Mrs. Webster answered. The Websters and the Harrisons had a nice, casual acquaintance, and she wanted to know all about Dave's mother, and how things were at the lake. By now Dave was very nervous indeed, and blurted, "Everything's great, Mrs. Webster, but I've got to talk to your husband!" She called him to the phone.

Mr. Webster was a hearty man with a booming voice. When Dave started to give him the story, the older man reacted just the way Dave had hoped he would. "What kind of lout laid traps on my land? Dave, I'd appreciate it if you'd get rid of those traps. I'll take the matter up with the young man the next time I get to Hobb Creek."

"I've already pulled the traps," Dave said.

"Good. You hang on to them, then. Don't give them back."

"I can't give them back because I threw them in the lake," Dave said.

"That's good, direct action! Then what's the problem, Dave? I'll have Mr. Richter get some 'No Trapping' signs and post them. Will that take care of it?"

"Not exactly," Dave said. "This Warden kid is so sore he wants my head on a platter."

"Would it help if I had a talk with the State Police?"

"No, because that would make a real federal case of it," Dave said.

"Then how about my calling the boy's father?

Is that the Mr. Warden at the Hobb Creek bank?

"I don't want you fighting my battles, Mr. Webster," Dave said.

"It's my battle too," Mr. Webster told him. "I think I'll put in a call right away, and I'll call you back after I've talked with Mr. Warden." Mr. Webster hung up.

Both Beth and Jim had been listening, and Jim started in, "We don't need all this talking. I'm going to ride to school with Davey tomorrow morning and take care of this Warden kid myself."

"That doesn't make any sense! You keep out of it!" Dave shouted.

Jim looked puzzled. Beth added to his puzzlement. She saw how really annoyed Dave was and suggested, "Jim, suppose you go to your room now and I'll go to my room too, so that Dave can handle this matter without our interference."

Jim was obviously angry and hurt, but he did as he was told. "I guess it's best if I leave too," Beth said uncertainly.

"No," Dave said, "you can stay. But thanks for getting rid of Jim."

"He means well," Beth said. "Don't be too hard on Jim. His intentions are good."

An hour went by before the telephone shrilled and Dave grabbed it. "I think the matter is settled,"

Mr. Webster said. "I told Mr. Warden I allowed no hunting or trapping on my land. I said the traps had been confiscated and that I approved of that action. He protested that he was sure his son hadn't set any traps illegally. My talk with the father doesn't take care of your problem, though, David. You have to meet the boy in school. Can you handle that end?"

"I'll have to," Dave said. "Thanks a lot, Mr. Webster."

"Keep me informed, hear?"

"Okay, Mr. Webster. Good night."

Beth had shut up the house and was holding Mose, ready to hand him over to Dave. They went upstairs, but she followed Dave into his room. "Dave, I'm scared stiff about tomorrow," she confessed. "Will you have anybody on your side, or will they line up with Bert?"

"I'll have Lew Collins." There weren't any ifs, ands, or buts about that. Lew would rise to the occasion. All through school he and Lew had stood side by side.

"He's even smaller than you are," Beth pointed out.

"He's small but he's tough. I may come home kind of bloody, but we'll worry about that tomorrow," Dave said. "Good night, Mom."

71

7

Dave awoke at six and heard rain pounding on the roof. The January thaw had arrived. It was dark as the inside of a cow, and Dave was depressed and scared enough already, without the weather adding to his troubles.

His mother was in the kitchen, poking up the fire. "Better rain than more snow," she said.

Jim might come bounding out of his room at any moment. Private conversations between Beth and Dave had to be sneaked in edgewise, these days, and Beth said hurriedly, "Did you know that Jim never even started high school? I talked to him about going to Regional but he refused. I thought that might be good for his morale."

"It wouldn't help his morale if he fell flat on his face because he couldn't hack it," Dave commented.

They let the matter drop, because both had the confrontation with Bert Warden on their minds.

There was no way to avoid getting on the school bus except by claiming sickness, and Dave saw no sense to that because the confrontation would only be delayed. He sprinted down the lane through a hard shower and waited, shivering, in the small shelter his father had built. It looked like those in pictures of Buckingham Palace, and they called it the sentry box. The yellow bus came in sight and he climbed aboard.

Lew was waiting outside for him when the buses arrived. He stuck like a burr to Dave's side all morning, but Dave didn't meet up with Bert until noon.

Again the encounter took place in the cafeteria. Dave and Lew were in the serving line, and Lew said in a low voice, "He's over there at the corner table."

Now that his fate was upon him Dave didn't know how to handle it. Should he stalk over and confront Bert directly? Should he let Bert make the move? He couldn't decide, so he and Lew took their trays to a table in the opposite corner.

Dave tried to eat as though this was any ordinary day, but the spaghetti and meatballs tasted like ground-up sawdust in his mouth. Lew warned him, "He's coming."

"Are any of the other kids with him?" Dave asked, not turning to look.

Lew didn't have time to answer. There Bert was, looking twice as large as life, his hands on his

73

hips. He was alone, but some of the eighth grade boys were gathering, sensing excitement. "I suppose if you've got a brother who steals cars, stealing traps doesn't seem like much!" Bert boomed out.

What Bert didn't know was that Mrs. Willower had appeared in the door at the far end of the big room. Well, it wasn't up to Dave to warn Bert to lower his voice. "I guess Mr. Webster called you," Dave said.

"He sure did; he talked to my dad. I suppose you think my dad lowered the boom on me? Well, he didn't; he's plenty sore too. He hopes you're taking care of those traps, because when we come to get them we'll have a State cop with us. I told my dad I was sure you'd be a good boy and hand them over polite and easy. Right, Dave?"

It would have solved Dave's problems if he could have handed over the traps, but he was just as glad he couldn't. Giving them back wouldn't solve the big problem, because then other animals would be caught in the wicked teeth. Dave found his voice. "Wrong," he croaked. "I'm not handing over no traps."

With that Bert was on him. He slapped Dave's face hard, jammed his elbow into Dave's midriff, then clutched Dave's shirt front in a big fist and lifted him off the floor. Scared as he was Dave had time to notice that the other boys had moved away. None of them were backing up Bert. He didn't see the principal until she spoke, directly behind Bert. "Put Dave down," she ordered calmly.

Bert hesitated, then did as he was told. Dave staggered, struggling to catch a deep breath.

"David, your grammar is very poor," Mrs. Willower went on. "You can't say, 'I'm not handing back no traps.' It has to be, 'I'm not handing back any traps.' We don't want double negatives, do we? And we don't want a fight in the cafeteria, either, do we? Bert, if you've finished your lunch, go take care of your tray and then leave this room. David, eat your lunch. We mustn't waste good food. And both of you keep out of the other's way." She waited until Bert went mooching off. Then she left.

Dave's lunch tasted like real food now. Lew went on and on excitedly about how great it was that the other boys had backed off.

On their way to room 41 Dave and Lew had to pass the office. Mrs. Willower stepped out, and Lew was still sticking so close he got his feet stepped on when Dave stopped short. "I heard the first part of that altercation," Mrs. Willower said. "Dave, I wanted to tell you I think it's wonderful that your half brother is living with you. If anyone can straighten him out, your mother can. Will you tell her that if I can help in any way, I'll be happy to do so?"

"Yes, ma'am," Dave mumbled.

The clock still had a couple of minutes to go before it bonged for the first afternoon class, and the boys waited in the hall. Lew was giving Dave odd looks. Finally he said, "I've got a funny feeling you don't think it's all that wonderful, Jim coming to live with you."

Dave had no answer. Instead he said, "How about coming out on my bus and having supper with us? My mother will drive you home, after."

"Great! I'll call my mother and tell her."

School ended at three. The rain had let up. The long line of buses was waiting to approach the entrance, and the kids were sorting themselves out for their buses. As the crowd parted, Dave saw a big, tow-haired boy sitting on the curb. Some of the eighth graders were looking at Dave knowingly. Why did Jim have to show up at school?

Jim jumped to his feet, a grin lighting up his face. "I wanted to make sure you're still in one piece, Davey," he said. "It looks like the guy didn't lay a finger on you."

76

He picked up two buckets. "I walked to town and got the caulking stuff for the boats," he explained. "They're kind of heavy, so I asked your bus driver and he said he'd give me a lift."

"Lew's coming, too," Dave told him.

Those two found seats together on the bus, and Dave stood close by. Lew was interested in Jim's project when Jim explained that he wanted to start getting the rowboats ready for spring. "We're thinking about opening up the lodge this summer," he told Lew.

"Who's 'we'?" Dave demanded sharply. This was news to him.

"Beth and I talked about it this morning, after you left," Jim told him. "I hauled one of the boats into the garage and started scraping. I figure I'll caulk them and then paint them. Red would be a good color. How about red, Davey?"

"Do you mean you might open up Journey's End and take in guests?" Lew asked.

"That's right."

Dave was getting mad now. "It's not up to you!" he snapped at Jim. "It's up to Mom. That's a tough job, taking guests. I know because Mom and I used to help Gramps Harrison when he ran the place."

"I'll be around to help," Jim said. "Maybe Lew would want to work for us. How about it, Lew? Do you want a job, next summer?"

"You shut up!" Dave ordered. "Don't try to fix everything all at once!"

Jim was startled, but he didn't take offense. He tried to soothe Dave, "Sure, sure, little brother."

Dave felt like yelling, "Stop calling me 'little brother'!" but he stopped in time. How could you snap at somebody who didn't snap back? Jim and Lew began talking about running the boat-hire part of the business, and Dave listened with half an ear, but he was thinking.

How were you supposed to talk to a guy who acted like an overgrown kid? Dave had adored Jim, years ago when they were both boys, but Jim wasn't any kid, now. Actually they were strangers to each other.

Lew changed the subject and asked about Burrows Rehabilitation Institute. It was obvious that Lew liked Jim. Jim answered frankly and said he'd met some wonderful guys at B.R.I., like his pal Cuffy. Dave and Lew would be crazy about Cuffy. He also had a counselor who was his real friend. They had free movies at the Institute and the food wasn't too bad, and they played a lot of handball. The only thing bad about the place was that you could never get out and run. Jim said maybe it bugged Dave, how he, Jim, got out and ran every chance he got. But Dave couldn't understand how great it was to feel free like that, to run on a road.

When they reached home Jim and Lew carried the caulking compound to the garage. Dave sought out his mother, who had just come in and was taking off her coat. Dave didn't know how to sneak into the subject so he plunged in. "Mom, how come you and Jim decided this morning you were going to open up Journey's End, next summer?"

"Jim suggested it but we didn't decide anything, Davey," she said.

"Oh," Dave said, and felt relieved. It had seemed to him that Jim was moving in on them and taking over.

"How could we decide a big thing like that without you?" Beth asked. "You and I are partners."

"Is Jim a partner too now?" Dave came out with what was on his mind. "It seems as though he's kind of taking over."

"Well, he isn't," Beth said. "He's a lot like your Dad, though. I mean, he's full of enthusiasm and he seems to enjoy making grandiose plans, the way your father did."

She hesitated. Then she added, "You and I were lucky, Dave. We had your father as a member of our family. Jim grew up without even knowing his father. So we have to make allowances for him. We'll take this thing one day at a time, and we'll be patient with Jim. Okay?"

"Okay," Dave said. He did agree, and added, "All right, I'll try harder. But I wish he wouldn't talk about that B.R.I. the way he does. I mean, the way he was talking to Lew Collins he made it sound as though it was a fancy prep school or something."

"When did he meet Lew?"

"Jim came home on the bus with us, he begged a ride off the driver. Oh, I forgot to tell you — Lew's staying for supper. All right?"

"Of course it is," Beth said. "Well now?" she challenged him.

" 'Well now' what?"

"Dave, I've had a terrible day. I've been scared to death that Bert Warden had beaten you into a bloody pulp!"

Dave grinned. "No, I'm not a bloody pulp. Bert never got around to beat up on me. He started a fight in the cafeteria, but he didn't have any back-up from the other kids, and the principal broke it up. She asked me to give you a message. She says she thinks it's fine that you took Jim to live with us."

"That's nice of Mrs. Willower," Beth said.

"Some people don't think it's all that wonderful."

"Like who?"

"Like Mrs. Morrill, who lives up past the Richters. The Richters think it's all right, but Mary Richter told me that Mrs. Morrill is saying people are in danger of being murdered in their beds. And our resident State policeman, Officer Delaney, isn't too keen. He sent me word that he'll come like a shot the first time Jim gets out of line ——" She broke off, because Jim and Lew were stamping their feet on the step, ready to come in.

She made chop suey for supper, so there was plenty for an extra guest. The talk was all about opening Journey's End next summer. Jim seemed to think it was all decided and everything was set. He made it sound as though they were ready to start taking guests right now, in the dark depths of winter.

Mrs. Harrison let him run on, but then she turned practical. "You boys can't imagine the amount of hard work that is involved," she said. "One woman couldn't do it, even with three good boys for assistants. It would mean hiring a cook, and also another woman to wait tables and help take care of the guest rooms."

"I'll bet there are lots of people who would be glad to get the work," Lew suggested.

"It's a chancy thing," Beth said dubiously. "It would cost a lot of money to stock the kitchen, buy linen, get the place in order. Journey's End has been closed for a long time, ever since Dave's grandfather got too old to run it. His customers used to come year after year; he never had to advertise. But we'd have to advertise."

"The fish are still here," Lew reminded her. "Enoch's Pond has always been the best fishing lake in the whole state. You don't have to buy boats, Mrs. Harrison. Jim and I are going to fix up the old ones. We'd run that end of the business."

"What about me?" Dave asked. "Am I supposed to be just sitting on my duff?"

"You and Mom would be the bosses," Jim said. "You'd tell everybody what to do."

"Grandfather Harrison catered just to the fishermen, who used to come alone and didn't care if things weren't fancy," Beth told them. "If their families came too, what would they do while the men were off fishing? This isn't exactly the most exciting place in the world!"

"They could swim," Lew said. "We'd clean up the beach. They could go to the drive-in movie, they could go to the summer theater in Northford. They could ride around and visit the gift shops. Hey, we might even have a gift shop here and sell souvenirs!"

Beth looked around the table. Maybe Dave looked doubtful, because he sure felt doubtful, but Lew's and Jim's faces were bright with enthusiasm. "I'm not going to commit myself and say yes, but we'll think about it," Beth promised.

8

THE BITTER COLD came back, and there was no snow on the ground to soften its impact. Even with the new insulation the ell was a shivery place, although the kitchen fire roared all the time. Would the cold ever lift? Mose was a smart cat, and hugged the fire. His leg was healed now, but he refused to venture outside.

Jim, too, could stay home all day, and he kept busy doing odd jobs, and did them fairly well. But Dave and his mother had to go out each morning and face zero cold. Jim's first job was to start Beth's car and leave it running until she was ready to leave. Sometimes she drove Dave to his school, but usually he took his own bus.

One morning he started down the lane, walking into a sharp wind that made the cold unbearable. He happened to glance across the frozen shore to the lake, and saw something that stopped him dead short.

Two large dogs had a deer down on the ice in the middle of the lake.

Dave ran back to the house yelling to his mother to get the revolver. Jim came to the door instead and Dave pushed by him, found the key, and unlocked the small drawer in the sideboard. The box of ammo was there, and he quickly loaded the .38.

Jim stood in his way. "What's up, kid?"

"Get out of my way!" Dave ordered.

"Listen, you can't use that thing!" Jim grabbed for the revolver, and they were wrestling for it when Beth interfered. Dave explained, and his mother ordered, "Let him go, Jim. He knows what he's doing."

The three ran to the shore. "Is the ice safe?" Beth asked.

"It's six inches thick," Dave told her.

"Leave the safety on until you get out there."

Dave couldn't stop Jim from following. The ice was glassy smooth, and it was lucky Dave obeyed his mother's warning because once he slipped and fell flat on his back, and if the gun hadn't been on the safety somebody might have got shot.

The dogs still had the deer down and it was frantically struggling to rise, but they held it by a rear leg, harrying it. Dave stopped, steadied himself, took off the safety, aimed over their heads.

Jim chose that moment to interfere. He got his hands on the barrel and yelled, "Let me! I'm oldest!"

"No!" Dave yelled back. "Hands off. I'm the one Dad taught to use this gun!"

Miraculously Jim obeyed, let go, and stepped back. "Sure, you were always his favorite, weren't you," he said sullenly.

That startled Dave. He had no idea Jim had felt that way.

"I bet you won't hit anything this far away," Jim said.

"I only want to warn them off," Dave told him.

He shot over the heads of the animals, and in the clear air the sound reverberated, bouncing off the hills. The dogs stopped, glanced toward shore. Dave let off another shot, and the way he felt he didn't care if he hit them. Maybe they were only doing what any big dogs on the run might do, but it was an awful thing to see.

They slouched off, then stopped, turned back. Dave let go a third shot, and that time they kept going toward the far shore, and disappeared into the underbrush.

The deer was floundering as Dave and Jim approached, trying to rise, its eyes wide with terror, fearful now of the boys and the gun. Dave saw that the tendons above the hoof were torn and the leg was partially bitten away. The creature got to its feet but collapsed, got to its feet again, starting slowly toward shore dragging the mangled leg. If it reached the shore it would only hide somewhere and die slowly.

Unless Dave acted.

He knew what he had to do; he had no choice. He aimed carefully as his father had taught him, aiming a little high. At first the finger on the trigger wouldn't obey because he had never in his life put a bullet into a living animal. He willed his forefinger to obey and the bullet went, the revolver's violent recoil throwing Dave's arm up. It struck in the neck. Jim was yelling, "Stop, stop!" but Dave glared at him to warn him. Dave aimed again, fired, and that time the bullet mercifully found the deer's head and the animal collapsed on the ice.

Dave slowly approached, ready to fire at close range. No, there was no life in the beautiful, dark eyes; they were starting already to glaze over.

Dave plodded toward shore, his head down. Jim tried to put an arm around him, but Dave said, "Please don't touch me." Beth took the revolver from his weak fingers. He had reached the shore when nausea overcame him, and he had to stop and heave up his breakfast.

When he was finished his mother handed Jim the revolver and took Dave's arm, leading him to the house. He was sweating and at the same time shivering with cold. They heard the school bus stop at the end of the lane, then go on. "I'll take you to school, but first I'll call the game warden," Beth said. She and Jim were anxiously watching Dave, being very gentle with him.

"He'll say we should have called him to do it," Dave said hoarsely.

"No. The deer would have escaped. Son, you did what you had to do. I know that's little comfort to you now, but it's true. You saved it hours, maybe days, of agony."

Dave dully listened while his mother talked on the phone. The warden argued, and she told him, "Come and see. You'll know too that my son acted correctly. I'm only asking you to take the deer away." She hung up on him.

They went out to the car and started toward town. Dave was holding himself together, he was doing fine, and then all of a sudden the whole thing got to him. Sobs shook him and he put his head down on the dashboard and cried helplessly. Beth stopped the car and gathered him in her arms and held him until he got control, murmuring, "There, there, there," smoothing back his hair as though he was a small child.

"It's okay," he muttered and straightened up.

She started the car and went on. 'David, you were entitled," she said. "You cried for the deer, not for yourself. Your dad would be very proud of you."

"He never used that gun to kill anything in his whole life."

"He would have done the same thing."

"He might have thought of something better than killing it."

"There wasn't anything better. Its leg was destroyed. It couldn't have survived. Son, there are worse things in this world than an easy death."

Beth's voice shook, and Dave knew she was thinking, "If only Joe Harrison himself could have been granted an easy death." They said no more, but she drove with one hand and they held hands tightly for the rest of the drive to town.

She went in with him, to explain to Mrs. Willower why he was late, and then went on to her own job.

Somehow Dave got through the day, but he wasn't really with it, his mind couldn't connect with what was going on in school. He briefly explained to Lew Collins what had happened. Bert Warden stopped him once and started to speak, but Dave gave him an ugly look and ordered, "Get out of my way!" and Bert backed off.

All the way home on the bus he was dreading

the moment when he would have to look toward the center of the lake. The driver let him off and he walked up the lane to the point where he had a clear view. The expanse of ice was empty. Only a dark shine of blood showed where the tragedy had taken place.

Thoughtfully, Jim had made cocoa, and he heated it up. "The warden came," he told Dave. "He said you did real good, Davey. He brought his truck down to the beach and we used ropes and hauled the deer over the ice and loaded it onto the truck."

"Thanks, Jim," Dave said. "For helping the warden, and for the cocoa and everything." The two were quiet together and at peace, there in the kitchen. Dave wished it could be that way all the time. Brothers ought to love each other. It was a waste of a good relationship if they were edgy with each other, ready to quarrel, he thought.

Jim, though, had something on his mind, and it came out that evening. "Dad taught Dave how to handle a gun. So why didn't he teach me?"

"You were only six years old, Jim, when your mother and father were divorced," Beth reminded him.

"But he came to see me."

"Of course he did, as often as he could," Beth

said. "He took you places, remember? When you were in New York he took you to the Zoo, and to Central Park, and to the Statue of Liberty, and out to dinner. He told me what good times you had together."

"Why didn't he take me to live with him?" Jim's eyes were somber, as though this question haunted him. "I was nuts about him. So if he liked me, why didn't he take me?"

Dave saw how carefully his mother was trying to answer. "Because he couldn't," Beth said. "I know how much he grieved over it, Jim. The court gave your mother custody, so he couldn't take you away from her."

"Then he stopped coming," Jim stated.

"Yes, because your mother was moving around the country, and most of the time he didn't know where you were. He did go out to Kansas City once, to see you."

"I remember," Jim said.

"Later, when you came to visit us here in Hobb Creek, your father was so happy!" Beth said. "He truly loved you, Jimmy. You mustn't ever doubt that."

There came a long pause. Then Jim reverted to the subject of the gun. "Why didn't he ever teach me how to use a gun? He taught Dave."

"Because you lived in different cities, and anyway, there's no point in city boys learning to handle guns." Jim thought that over, shrugged, and dropped the subject.

He didn't lose interest in the gun, however. Once Dave came upon him holding it, sighting along the barrel. Nowadays, Dave could forget sometimes that his brother was an ex-con, but seeing Jim holding the gun sharply reminded him. "How did you find the key to the drawer?" he asked.

"I saw where you put it."

"Come on, Jim, let's put the gun back."

Jim did so reluctantly. Then he spied a small box in the drawer which held Beth's most cherished possession, the ring Joe Harrison had given her, a sapphire surrounded by diamonds. Jim put it on his finger, studied it. "Neat," he said. "What's this?" He unfolded the tissue from Joe Harrison's wrist watch, a fine, thin Swiss watch.

"It was Dad's," Dave explained.

Jim's face was stony. "What's the matter, Jim?" Dave asked.

"Dad never gave me a watch," Jim mumbled.

"He didn't give me one either," Dave said. "It isn't mine. It's just there, in the drawer. Come on, Jim, let's lock this stuff up again." They did so, and Dave took the key. He had an impulse to unlock the drawer and give the watch to Jim and say, "Here, you can have it." He didn't do that, though, because the watch wasn't his to give. It belonged to Beth.

The incident bothered Dave in another way, too. He hadn't liked the eager look on Jim's face when Jim handled the gun. Dave hid the drawer key in a new place, under the dish towels in the towel drawer.

If Jim questioned his security as a member of the family he didn't show it again. He threw himself into the job of getting Journey's End ready for the summer. He put on warm clothes and started cleaning the main lodge.

He still had a lot of time on his hands, though. His life was unsupervised because Beth and Dave were away at school so much of the time. He got into the habit of going to town, either hitching a ride, or walking. Not that he often walked; he usually ran the four miles to Hobb Creek.

He grew restless. He was a gregarious boy who made friends easily. There weren't many boys his age in Hobb Creek who had free time on their hands, as he did; most of them worked. Hobb Creek didn't have any pool halls or places like that, but it had two gas stations, and Jim found friends there.

Dave and Beth began to get reports about his hanging around the gas stations, just socializing, drinking Cokes, kidding with the customers, sometimes helping with repair jobs. He was so open and friendly, people liked him. It bothered Beth that he was spending so much time away from home, but it was impossible for her and Dave to ride herd on him all the time, and he wasn't breaking the law, doing anything wrong.

Jim rarely mentioned his mother, but when her name came up his eyes turned dark and somber. Dave got the impression he had some really ugly memories of her. Jim had no such feeling about B.R.I, though. He spoke often of the place and apparently he had been really happy there. Once in a while when he felt lonesome he talked on the phone with his pal Cuffy. "He was the best cellmate I ever had," he told Dave. Finally one day he put in a long-distance call to his pal, and Cuffy's mother told him that Cuffy had been re-arrested and sent back to the Institute.

Dave and his mother were vaguely aware of what was going on in Jim's mind, but they were completely taken by surprise by what he did. Afterward they pieced the story together this way. Jim had thought his problem through and decided that if he had gotten himself into Burrows before by swiping a car, he could do it again. He showered and dressed in clean clothes, then trotted to Hobb Creek. At the supermarket parking lot he hung around until he saw a woman get out of her car, leaving the key in the ignition. As soon as she was inside the store Jim got in the car and took off.

He didn't go joy-riding or anything like that, although Dave suspected he felt very happy having a set of wheels under him. He drove straight to the house of the resident State cop, Officer Delaney, on Main Street in Hobb Creek, then parked in front of the house and sat and waited.

The woman came out of the store with her groceries and found her car gone and called the State Police. They in turn called Officer Delaney. He was out on patrol, and didn't answer his radio, so they called his wife and she took the information. While she was talking to the lieutenant at the State barracks she happened to glance out her window and said, "There's a car parked in front of our house that answers the description." She went to a window where she could see the license plate, and it tallied.

About this time Officer Delaney called in on his radio and learned the story and went straight home. The car was still there with Jim behind the wheel waiting to be arrested. The cop obliged him and took him to the barracks and booked him.

The Harrisons got into the story then, for Lieutenant Thorne called Beth at the high school. She was totally unprepared and shocked at the news.

Once again she picked up Dave at his school, and they drove to see Jim in jail, only this time it was to the barracks on the state road instead of the police station in Northford. Lieutenant Thorne in the meantime had learned about Jim's prior arrests for car theft, and he was very confused.

He invited Beth and Dave into his private office where he tried to get them to explain the case to him. "Why does he use the same M.O.?" he asked. "He wanted to be arrested, and stole that car for that sole purpose."

"That seems to be the case," Mrs. Harrison said. "As for the why, I wish we knew."

"He missed some guy named Cuffy, and his other pals," Dave put in. "He likes that place in Burrows. He wanted to go back. Lately he's talked about it as though it was the greatest place on earth."

"Well, I'm afraid this time it won't go so easily with him," the lieutenant said. "He's nineteen now, and he's got two priors. With two priors, and at his age, the judge may send him to State Correctional."

"But that's not what Jim wants!" Dave exclaimed. Then he shut up, realizing how silly that sounded.

"He's an awfully nice boy," Beth said. "We're very fond of him, aren't we, Dave?" Dave nodded. "He probably needs professional psychiatric help,"

Beth went on. "Is there any chance he will get that at the State prison?"

"I don't know," the lieutenant said, "but I doubt it."

Jim was brought out then, to say good-bye to them. Dave expected he would look roughed up, because State Police were supposed to be a tough lot, but no, he seemed fine. His face didn't wear its usual happy expression, though, and he seemed very serious and scared. He gently kissed Beth, started to shake hands with Dave, changed his mind and kissed him too. "Oh Jim, why did you do it?" Beth cried.

Jim seemed to be trying hard to be honest with her, and with himself too. "I don't rightly know, Beth. I guess the case is, I just couldn't hack it out there."

"But you were doing fine! We were making plans. You were the one who wanted to open up the lodge. You seemed so happy."

"I was!"

"So why did you do it?"

Jim stared at his shoes for a long time. Then he said in a low voice, "I guess I never really felt I belonged, there at the lodge. You and Dave were wonderful to me, but I never felt like part of the family."

"Of course you are," Dave protested weakly.

They waited, but Jim said no more. Nobody mentioned that he might not get back to Burrows to rejoin his friends, he might be sent to the State prison.

Somebody had to break up this painful scene. "We'll keep in touch," Dave said.

Jim looked relieved. "I wish you would, Dave. And hey, when you and Lew put the boats in, this spring, let them soak good, so the wood swells. Then haul them out again and check the seams where I caulked, and then give the bottoms another coat of paint. The man at the hardware store said that was the right way, the safe way. You can't rent them if they leak."

"Okay, will do," Dave told him.

Jim folded Beth in his long arms again, muttered, "Mom, I'm awful sorry," and bolted out of the office.

Lieutenant Thorne walked with the Harrisons to their car. "This case has really got to me," he admitted.

"Will they be kind to him, at the State prison?" Beth asked.

"Well, Mrs. Harrison, nobody would claim it's exactly a pleasure resort."

"Will we be able to go to see him?"

"Yes, but the rules about visiting are strict."

"Can we be present at his trial? I could testify that he's a good boy."

"If you want to come, fine. I'll call you when the date is set."

They left and started home. Dave was remembering that other day when they had driven home to Hobb Creek, leaving Jim to his fate. Dave felt confused and miserable. A real conviction was growing in his mind, though, and he had to let it out. "Mom," he said, "I wonder if we ought not to drop the whole thing."

"What do you mean, Dave?" Beth turned to him, surprised.

"I mean, you did your best. I did too, and maybe my best wasn't very good, but I tried. I wish Jim would shape up, but maybe he just can't. He said himself he couldn't hack it, out in the real world. Maybe we ought to just let him go."

She drove a mile or two. Then she said, "David, I'm sorry, but I can't do that. There's something awfully lovable about Jim, and he's so terribly alone in the world. And he is Joe Harrison's son."

9

ONCE AGAIN the *Northford News* picked up the story of Jim's arrest. The Harrisons had a few bad days. Bert Warden announced loudly during basketball practice, "I see they busted that wonderful brother of Dave's again." Mrs. Richter called to say that she and her husband and their girls liked Jim, and were truly sorry. When Beth and Dave went to town to gas up the pickup truck the people at the gas station also said they were sorry.

Lew told Dave, "That's tough, about Jim."

"Yeah, tough," Dave said briefly.

"What happens about the rental business?"

"You can come out and help me run it this summer, if you want to," Dave told him.

"Jim really put those boats in good shape."

"Yeah."

"He's quite a guy. Do you know why he got himself back in the can?"

"No."

"You don't want to talk about it," he guessed.

"That's right," Dave said.

The days went along, and gradually the thought of Jim slipped to the back of Dave's mind. In mid-March a blizzard struck and buried the area in snow. It drifted and choked the lane. It was too much for Dave to handle, and even Mr. Richter's plow couldn't handle it, so Dave and his mother were snowbound. The power went off, but luckily the generator was working, and they switched over to it. Jim had put it in beautiful condition.

Jim's trial took place the day the storm hit, and of course they didn't get there. Mrs. Harrison called the State Police barracks and learned that Jim had been sentenced to four to six months in the State prison. Lieutenant Thorne told her that with time off for good behavior he would be out in about three months, and the lieutenant asked if she intended to take Jim back when his time was up. Beth gave him a vague answer to the effect that she didn't know.

She began writing letters to Jim, but she and Dave rarely mentioned him. They were both confused by his strange behavior, and Dave sensed that his mother was deeply hurt. Sometimes Dave felt relieved because the burden of his brother had been lifted from him, but other times he had sharp pangs of regret, and even missed Jim.

A cold front with zero weather moved down out of Canada, and it was a struggle just to survive those days of being snowbound, just to get in enough wood and to keep tolerably warm. The Harrisons blessed Mr. Garcia. The ell was so flimsy, they would surely have frozen to death if he hadn't insulated it.

Like all local people they knew enough to keep a supply of food on hand against such an emergency. Just the same they ran out of a few necessities. To make matters worse, on the third day the telephone line went dead, so they had no contact with the outside world.

After the first few days Dave began to feel stir-crazy. He got an inkling of what Jim's life behind bars and high walls was like, and why, when Jim got out, he had to run. Dave felt like breaking through the door and running, but that was impossible when the drifts were so high.

He had never learned to use snowshoes well, but finally he couldn't stand it any longer, being shut up in the house with his mother and Mose. He had heard the town plows working on the main road, and announced to Beth he was going to try to reach the Richters to borrow some milk and bacon and eggs. She argued, but he said, "Just think how bacon and eggs would taste." He went outside into the still cold and tied on his new snowshoes.

His mother watched from the door. "Would you check the northwest corner?" she called. "There's a blast of cold air coming up through the floor there."

The ell had no cellar, only a crawl space so air could circulate. Dave plodded to the corner his mother mentioned and saw that a passage had been made through the snow and the cornstalks which were piled against the foundation. He sniffed.

His mother was still waiting at the door, and he told her, "We've got company. Skunks. I'd say, from the tracks, there's more than one."

"If we don't bother them they won't bother us," she said, and shut the door.

Dave slogged down the lane, thinking his mother was really kind of flaky. She didn't turn a hair because a family of skunks had taken up residence under the house. Most women would panic. It was lucky that Mose hugged the fire and refused to go outside. If Mose got nosy and followed the tracks under the house he would get doused but good, and they would have to share their quarters with a skunk-y cat. You could bathe a dog in tomato juice, if it took a direct hit, but how would you get the stink off a long-haired cat?

By the time he reached the end of the lane his knees and ankles were killing him. Sure enough, the main road was clear, and he took off the snowshoes. A quarter of a mile up the road he discovered why the telephone line was down: A dead elm had toppled across the wires.

At the Richters he received an enthusiastic welcome, and he and Louise congratulated each other because there was no school. Mrs. Richter made him sit down at the kitchen table, and cooked him a marvelous meal of sausage and pancakes.

When he mentioned that the Harrisons had no phone, Mrs. Richter suggested he call the selectmen. "They probably don't know you're snowbound," she said. "Your ma has an important job, so she's got to get out."

"Do you mean they might plow a private road?" Dave asked.

"Why don't you try it? You pay taxes, and this is a good chance to see if a taxpayer can get something back, for all that money."

Dave got a response he didn't expect. The first selectman said, "Good grief, it never occurred to us you folks were shut in. I'll make sure the big plow's out there before nightfall."

Dave thanked him and hung up. "People are nice," he told Mrs. Richter.

"People aren't too awful," she agreed.

Louise, who was in Dave's class at school, was

pretty, but Emily, who was eighteen, was beautiful. Dave always had a tough time when he was near her because he was afraid he stared at her like a love-sick calf. His hands got sweaty and he shook inside. Now she poured him another cup of coffee and sat down with him. "What do you hear from Jim?" she asked.

He hesitated. "You don't want to talk about it," she said.

"No, that's all right," Dave said. "We haven't heard anything, Em. We didn't get to the trial; it was the day the storm struck. Jim got four to six months in the State prison. My mother's started sending him letters, but we haven't had too much time to think about it. These past few days it's been kind of hard just to take care of ourselves. I mean, we're beginning to get awfully sick of beans!"

He felt embarrassed about taking food after the big breakfast he had just eaten, but Mrs. Richter insisted on loading his knapsack with bacon, eggs, milk, and fresh bread she had baked that morning.

His mother was watching at the kitchen window when he came in view. Somehow, she looked very small and lonely, standing there and hoping for the sight of him. She was a gutsy woman, he could depend on that, and sometimes he forgot that she was also very lonely, and not too strong.

His greeting was hearty when he opened the door. "Hey, I'm back, and have I got food!" She hugged him, looking relieved and happy, and he realized he had been a real silent and morose character, lately.

She cooked up a nice feast of bacon and eggs and fried potatoes for supper. Dave was trying to be more companionable, so he agreed when she suggested they ought to send some gifts to Jim. Maybe he would have liked to forget Jim, because the thought of his brother was like a dull ache, but he went along. "Sure, whatever you say, Mom."

The plow came that night as the selectman had promised, and the next day the Harrisons finally got to town — Dave to school, Beth to her teaching job. She was late reaching home; she had been shopping for Jim.

They wrapped the gifts carefully, the same as last time, candy, chewing gum, paperback books, and packed them in a carton, which Beth mailed the next day. A week later the package was returned, with a form letter stating that inmates were not allowed to receive gifts from outside. If a person wished, he could send money to be credited to the inmate's account at the commissary, where he could draw upon it. The letter gave Jim's prison number, 86452.

Beth sadly unwrapped the packages. "Here,

Dave, you can have the candy. I'll put the other things in Jim's room, and I'll send a check for twenty-five dollars."

"Do you think he'll ever be back?" Dave asked.

"I don't know. Do you want him to come back, Dave?"

"I don't know what I want," Dave said, trying to be honest. "I mean, he brings an awful lot of trouble along with him."

"Perhaps we'd be smart to put him out of our minds," his mother said, her voice trembling.

March passed, and the turning year was swinging up toward spring. A real thaw came, not the temporary kind they got in the dead of winter. One evening Dave wandered down to the lake. The ice was gone and Enoch's Pond looked dark and oily in the pale light of the half moon.

At last the spot where the deer had died had vanished forever, with the melted ice. Dave stood stock still, recalling that terrible day. He wasn't thinking of the deer he had killed, though, he was thinking of Jim, how he had put Jim down when they wrestled for the revolver, how coldly he had spoken, how he had used his authority because he was Joe Harrison's accepted son. He thought how Jim had been pushed around all his life — and yet he came up sunny, affectionate, friendly.

"If Jim ever does come back I'll try to be nicer," he made up his mind.

Beth made one trip to see Jim. This time Dave didn't go; Mr. Richter took her. She didn't have much to say about the experience, except that she'd been allowed to talk to Jim for fifteen minutes through a wire screen, and that Jim seemed to be in good health. Dave didn't question her because she seemed really shaken, and he gathered that the experience of going to a State prison had been a hairy one.

There were more freezeups and more thaws, and March passed, and April. The trees were leafing out. They removed the cornstalks piled around the foundation, and when the cornstalks were gone the skunks departed, making life a little less uncertain. It was good to step outside and know you weren't going to confront a skunk that might take offense and whirl and squirt.

Mr. Richter plowed a plot of ground for a vegetable garden. There wasn't any way to pay Mr. Richter for all his kindness; the Harrisons could only accept it and be grateful. He asked, though, why Beth wanted the work of taking care of a garden, when the Richters were glad to give her all the vegetables she could use. She told him she was thinking of opening Journey's End in a limited way.

His red, sweaty face glowed with pleasure at this

news. "That's fine, Beth! But the fishing season starts in two weeks. You won't be ready by then."

"No, but there'll be good fishing all summer. You know Enoch's Pond — it's so full of fish they're practically standing on each other's backs. I wonder if Emily would like to work here full time, starting in June. I'd insist on paying her a fair wage, of course."

"I think Emily will be pleased, and she'll give you a fair day's work for what you pay."

"I'm sure of that," Beth said. "You and Mary have done a wonderful job raising those girls."

Hiring Emily was okay with Dave; it would be great just having her around to look at. He knew, though, that he would have to be very careful not to let his face show how he really felt about her.

He discussed with Beth the idea of hiring Lew, too, to run the boat rental business and to take on some of the chores which were going to fall on Dave's shoulders. Beth agreed.

Lew was only waiting to be invited, and jumped at the chance. He came the following Saturday to spend the day. He and Dave worked out a system of rollers and hauled the twelve boats from the garage down to the water's edge. The bottom seams leaked, but they would close as the wood expanded.

Jim had done a good job, and they looked fine, gleaming red with a white stripe along the gunwales.

Lew suggested they paint numbers on the bows so they could keep records of which fisherman took which boat and for how many hours. Mrs. Harrison said they'd do it right, and she would buy aluminum numbers to be attached to the bows.

They started a garden. Dave knew nothing about gardening, so Mr. Richter instructed him. After he gave the piece of ground another thorough plowing, he told Dave what to plant; then Dave and Lew put in corn, beans, tomatoes, peppers, and eggplant.

Now it was warm enough to open up the main inn. They aired it out and Beth began working there on weekends and also on weekdays after she got home from school. She was opening only ten rooms, but each had to be scrubbed thoroughly. Some of the furniture and woodwork had to be repainted. Dave worked along with her, and Emily helped each weekend.

Even with all the help, though, Beth began to look thin and drawn. "Mom, you can't keep on working this way," Dave finally said. "You're getting skinny as a rail."

"How about you?" she said. "You're skinnier than a rail, you're skinny as a lath. You work just as hard."

"If we do get guests, there'll be all the cooking to

do, on top of everything else. I don't see how you can hack it."

"I know we'll have to hire a cook," she said.

"Who?"

"Miss Samantha Flint, your dad's old friend."

"Oh no!" Dave said.

"Oh yes," his mother said. "Besides being the world's best Latin teacher she's also one of the world's best cooks. Don't you remember those marvelous nut bars she made for you at Christmas? I'll bet she'd jump at the chance."

"Mom, she's about a hundred and ninety years old!"

"She's in her seventies, and as lively and capable as a woman half her age. Honestly, Davey, you'll adore her when you get to know her."

The Harrisons drove to Miss Flint's house in town, and Beth asked her. Sure enough, Miss Flint grabbed at the chance. Maybe she was getting on in years, she said, but she wasn't afraid of wearing out; she was only afraid of rusting out. She would move to Journey's End a week before opening day, the fifteenth of June. That was the Monday after school closed, when Dave and Beth would at last be free.

Now that all the plans were set, Beth put advertisements in a Boston paper and a New York paper. She also sent notices of the inn's reopening to several hundred people who had been guests in the old days, when Dave's grandfather ran the place.

At first Beth and Dave worried that there would be no replies and that all their hard work would come to nothing. Then requests for reservations began to arrive. They hadn't miscalculated — Enoch's Pond was still famous as one of the best fishing lakes in the Northeast. With great excitement they realized they had better start worrying instead about getting too many bookings.

Everything was set for Monday, the fifteenth of June. The fleet of bright little boats bobbed along the dock. The raft was painted and anchored. Lew and Dave policed the grounds, making the whole place neat and shipshape. The inn's refrigerators bulged with food. Miss Samantha Flint moved in, and Beth was right, Dave began to be crazy about the perky old lady.

The bedrooms and public rooms were ready and Emily looked lovely in her new blue uniform. She fussed over the dining room, which was her special domain, arranging linen and dishes and silver, collecting vases for the wildflowers with which she planned to decorate.

Beth was everywhere at once, with a hundred jobs to do simultaneously, but she looked happy and alive, the way she used to look before her husband died.

And then on the Saturday morning before opening day the telephone shrilled. Dave answered it in the ell and his mother picked up the phone in the lobby. They hoped it was somebody wanting a reservation, because they still had two rooms open.

No, it was Jim. "Hey," he yelled, "I'm out!"

10

THERE WAS SILENCE on the Hobb Creek end of the line. "Is anybody there?" Jim called.

"Yes, we're here," Beth said. "That's fine, Jim."

"Could I come home? I left some stuff, and I want to pick it up."

"Yes, of course," Beth said.

"I'm only going to stay one night," Jim told her. "Brother, are you there?"

"Yes, I'm here," was all Dave could find to say.

"I'll see you. I'm thumbing my way and I'll be home tonight."

Dave went to his mother and found her sitting in a wicker chair in the lobby, looking helpless and happy both at the same time. "Oh dear," she said, "we never run out of complications, do we?"

"He said he was staying only one night."

"We'll just have to do the best we can," Beth

said. "Let's hope Jim's visit is pleasant. Let's try to *make* it pleasant." Dave nodded.

Both of them were too busy that day to spend much time worrying. Dave had promised to help Lew with a major project. Lew had big plans for the rental business. Out of scraps of boards he and Dave had cobbled together a hut for the end of the dock. Lew's new authority had gone to his head, and he had made a sign and tacked it over the door of the hut, "DOCK MASTER."

It worried him that in a wind the boats could bang against each other, scarring their paint. This morning the boys' job was to drive poles paralleling the dock, so that the boats could be tied both bow and stern. The lake shelved off gradually, so Dave could stand in the water and work. He held each pole, while Lew hung over the stern of the rowboat and pounded the pole into the sandy bottom with a maul. Lew's arms soon gave out because the maul was heavy, so they reversed jobs and he held the pole while Dave pounded.

They worked along both sides until twelve poles were set and the boats were bobbing gently, safely secured. "That looks more shipshape," Lew commented.

He went on to elaborate a new idea. "Out of the profits we could start buying outboard motors, one at a time," he suggested. "Maybe we could pick them up secondhand. If the boats had motors we could charge double."

He went on and on about this new idea, but Dave just grunted, "Sure, sure." Finally Lew accused him, "You didn't hear anything I said."

"Jim's coming tonight," Dave said. "I guess I was thinking about that."

"He's out? That's great!" Then the enthusiasm faded from Lew's face and he said, "If Jim's here then he'll be dock master."

"Oh no, nothing like that," Dave assured Lew. "He'll only be here one night."

"You don't particularly want him to come."

Dave didn't answer. After a while Lew asked, "You're not afraid of him, are you?"

The question startled Dave. He had never thought of that angle. "No, of course not," he said.

"I mean, because he's kind of big, he's a big, powerful guy."

"I'm not afraid of him," Dave said, and Lew tactfully shut up.

Doing their own work kept Dave and his mother apart, and they had little time to discuss Jim's arrival. Miss Flint, however, cornered Dave in the inn kitchen. "Your ma tells me your brother is coming here, fresh out of prison," she said. "It bodes no good, David. No good at all." Dave left because he didn't want to argue.

He looked for Emily and found her putting the final touches on the dining room. He stopped short. "Em, it looks really great!"

It did, too. The waxed floor gleamed, the tables for four in their new blue tablecloths looked inviting, the silver and glasses shone. Everything was ready, but Emily was saying distractedly, "With all I've still got to do before tomorrow night, how will I ever find time to set my hair?"

"Listen, only two parties are booked for tomorrow night," Dave reminded her. "The rest aren't due until Monday."

"I hear Jim's coming."

"That's right."

"Well, I for one will be glad to see him," Emily said. "He's an awfully nice boy." The way she said "awfully nice boy" made it sound as though Jim was younger than she, instead of a year older. It crossed Dave's mind that he'd like to hear her speak as warmly as that about himself. But if Jim seemed young to her, then he, Dave, must seem like only a little kid. And what chance did he have with her anyway, when every male in Hobb Creek considered her the prettiest girl for miles around?

Lew finished his work and rode his bike back to

town, and Emily finished and went home to wash her hair. Miss Flint had spent the day making pies and cakes and stuff for the guests, but she had cooked a bang-up dinner for Beth and Dave. She made them eat in the inn kitchen so they wouldn't mess up Emily's dining room.

The three were enjoying their food, not talking because they were exhausted. They heard steps in the lobby, somebody calling, "Anybody home?" and Jim pushed through the swinging door.

Beth went to him and he grabbed her. He hugged Dave, too, but Dave wriggled out of the embrace. His brother didn't smell like the old Jim, of soap and fresh air, he smelled sour. Was that the prison odor?

Miss Flint was introduced, and Jim didn't bat an eye because she was so ancient. She looked properly scandalized because she was entertaining a convict in her kitchen, but that didn't stop her from telling him severely that if he wanted to sit down and share their dinner he would have to wash up first.

The conversation was jerky; nobody knew what to say. What could you say to somebody just out of prison? Dave watched Jim covertly, trying to figure out how he was changed. Jim looked flabby, he had lost his lean, hard, healthy look. His expression was different. He had always smiled easily, but now he didn't smile. He said cheerful things, telling about the people who had given him rides. But even when he looked straight at you his eyes didn't focus right. The bright shine was gone out of them.

They finished eating, and while Beth helped Miss Flint tidy the kitchen, Dave took Jim around to see all the changes in the place. Jim marveled at the job they had done, getting the inn ready. They wandered down to the dock.

They were standing at the end of the dock. Jim admired the way Dave and Lew had tethered the boats. Then he said in a low voice, "You're not glad I came, Davey, and neither is Ma."

What else could Dave say? "Sure we are!" he protested.

They all needed their rest and went to their rooms early. Before she went to bed, though, Beth came in to speak to Dave. "What do you think, Dave?"

"I don't know, Mom."

"We have no idea what kind of experiences he's had in prison," she said. "We don't know what kind of men he's met. Those are tough men up there. It's a tough place. I know, I saw it. I don't like Jim's eyes. There's something in them. I just don't know — it scares me. You too?"

"No," Dave said, "he doesn't scare me."

"That's good, I'm glad to hear that," she said, and went to her own room.

When Dave straggled downstairs on Sunday morning he found Jim working outside, edging the shrubbery in front of the inn. Dave looked around. Jim must have been at it since daybreak, for the stone path to the dock looked very neat, and even the boulders which were outcropping on the lawn were made tidy.

Jim didn't look up, he was so intent on driving the edger to make a neat line. "Hey, that looks great!" Dave said, putting his hand on Jim's shoulder clumsily, trying to be affectionate.

Jim gave him a grin. "Glad you like it, little brother! I learned upstate. They let me work on an outside detail."

Beth gave the boys their breakfast. Nothing was said about Jim's leaving, and he went back to his job. When he finished the edging he tackled the garage, swept it out, arranged the tools. He found a half gallon of yellow paint and the next thing Dave knew he was painting Lew's dock shack. He went on that way all day long, not talking to anybody, working as though the furies were driving him. Miss Flint admitted to Dave, "He may be a jailbird but he's a wonderful worker."

He was respectful to Miss Flint, he was attentive

to Beth, and his eyes followed Emily wherever she went. Well, no wonder. Emily's cornflower eyes were so blue and she was so friendly and sweet and natural, how could anybody not want to look at her?

Dinner time came. Two parties had arrived early, and Beth had registered them, and Dave and Lew had carried their bags to their rooms. Now Emily was giving them their dinner in the dining room.

Dave and his mother were behind the lobby desk, contentedly listening to the clatter of dishes and the pleasant sound of voices in the dining room, when Jim sought them out. "I guess I ought to stay for a week or so, until everything gets going good," he said, sounding very nervous.

Beth somehow got up the courage to say, "I don't know about that, Jim. We were badly disappointed, the last time you got into trouble."

"Nothing like that will happen, Mom."

Beth appealed to Dave, "What do you think?"

What else could he say? "I guess," Dave said.

"Are you on probation?" Beth asked.

"Yes," Jim said. "I'd be in awful trouble if I got out of line. So I won't get out of line."

"All right. But if things begin to go sour, Jim, I'll have to ask you to leave."

The next morning guests began arriving by car,

and by lunch time Journey's End was a very busy place. Dave had forgotten what the inn was like when his grandfather was running it. In Gramps Harrison's day most of the guests had been fishermen who left their families at home, but now the ten rooms which were opened were occupied by married couples, and Dave had set up cots for those who brought children. In all, there were twenty-five people to be fed and bedded down and kept amused. Dave was surprised to learn how noisy little kids were, how the boys yelled and the little girls shrieked.

Everybody, and that included Lew, had to pitch in and help get the dinner served. Jim worked with Emily, carrying in the heavy trays, removing dirty dishes. Miss Flint ruled her kitchen like a sergeant major. Beth worked right alongside her. Lew and Dave ran everywhere at Miss Flint's command; she really ran them ragged. She was having a fine time, rushing around like a young girl instead of a seventy-two-year-old woman.

This first night she was serving roast beef and Yorkshire pudding, and she was such a marvelous cook the guests were eating everything in sight. The staff was supposed to have their dinner after the guests had finished, but tonight there wouldn't be anything left. This didn't help Lew's and Dave's morale because the roast beef and Yorkshire pudding smelled good and they were starving.

To cap the climax the ancient dishwasher pooped out while the first load was going through. Jim dropped what he was doing and with the boys' help pulled it away from the wall and attacked its interior. Dave had forgotten that Jim was some kind of a genius with motors. He scurried around finding tools as Jim barked orders. Beth washed dishes at the sink, and Emily helped when she found a few free minutes.

The pie and coffee were served, and after a while the dining room was empty and silent. Lew made himself a peanut butter sandwich and left, because some of the guests wanted to fish in the twilight. They had free use of the boats; only outsiders who wanted to fish Enoch's Pond would pay. Just the same, Lew had to be on the dock to help the guests get started. He figured that in some cases he would have to show them how to row.

Dave, too, staved off starvation with a peanut butter sandwich, while he stood by Jim, handing tools. Jim emerged from the back of the dishwasher and wiped his greasy hands and said with satisfaction, "Now she'll go."

He was right; when they loaded the washer and pressed the button it quietly did its job. At last, order began to be restored. Emily tidied the dining room and came out to wait for clean dishes so she could set up for breakfast. Beth collapsed at the big work table, but Miss Flint was still fresh as a rose and bustled around scrambling eggs and frying sausage for the working staff.

Ten o'clock came. The kitchen was again immaculate. Miss Flint eyed the clock and said, "This is much too late for an old lady like me to be getting to bed," and departed for her room. Lew soon left for town on his bike, and Jim drove Emily home in the pickup.

Dave saw that his mother didn't like this. She and he were alone now, in the inn kitchen. Dave didn't like it either, but he said, "Em will be okay. She can take care of herself."

"It's a terrible thing, but I'm afraid I just don't trust Jim," Beth admitted. "He's a changed boy from the one we used to know. Have you noticed, Dave? He hardly ever smiles now, or if he does his eyes don't smile. He's worked awfully well today, though. Maybe we'll begin to build up confidence in him."

They were both content to sit quietly, resting. After a while Beth spoke about hiring another helper for meal times, and also a part-time assistant for Dave, to keep up the grounds. Dave had figured on

Lew helping with the mowing and taking care of the vegetable garden, but Lew was so absorbed in his own job Dave feared he would never be able to pry him away from the dock. "We can't hire extra help, though, until a little time has gone by and we're sure the business is going to turn a profit," Beth pointed out.

She and Dave made a tour of the place at eleven o'clock. The last fisherman came in, and Dave helped him tie up. Then he and his mother went to their own quarters.

Jim was in his room; he hadn't sought them out to say good night, but he was home, and that was a relief. They heard him moving about behind his closed door.

At the top of the stairs Beth paused. "I feel so uneasy," she said. "I wish Jim would talk about what it was like, in prison, so we'd get everything out in the open. Well, for that matter, I've always wished he'd talk about his life with Nina. We could cope with Jim better if we knew him better."

"Maybe he'll change back to the way he used to be," Dave said. "You know. Happy-like."

"Let's hope so," Beth said. "Good night, son."

11

IT WAS PROBABLY LUCKY that the Harrisons had to work so hard, during those days of early summer. They didn't have time to worry about what people were thinking. Lew reported that people in town were talking about Jim coming back to the inn, but Lew was still crazy about Jim and defended him every chance he got. Once, after Beth went to the bank, she told Dave that the tellers were friendly, but Mr. Warden, the vice president, seemed hostile, and stopped her to warn her about taking in an ex-con. Dave pointed out that probably the Wardens were still sore about the loss of the traps.

Beth and Dave couldn't discount it, though, when the resident State cop came out to the inn to talk to them. Dave saw Officer Delaney parking his black-and-white car in the space reserved for guests, and steered him to the inn kitchen, where Beth was helping prepare lunch.

"Lieutenant Thorne asked me to come, to talk about the older Harrison boy," Officer Delaney began.

He glanced at the cook, who was stirring a soup pot on the stove. "Anything we have to say we can say in front of Miss Flint," Beth assured him.

He laughed. "I've been out of school for fifteen years, but I'm still scared of Miss Flint," he admitted.

"You weren't in my Latin classes, so what were you afraid of?" Miss Flint demanded.

"You tutored me in algebra one summer. Don't you remember?"

"Of course I remember. You were the Delaney boy with the thick skull. I had to pound algebra into it with a mallet."

Miss Flint served them coffee and joined them at the table. "Did you come here to harass Jim?" she asked.

"No, Miss Flint. But he's done time in prison, so, like the lieutenant says, we have to keep an eye on him."

"He's courteous, and he does his work, and the guests like him," Miss Flint stated.

"Have any of his friends from upstate contacted him?" the office asked.

Beth told him no. Dave kept his mouth shut, but he knew this wasn't so. Beth wasn't aware of it, but once, late at night, Jim had sneaked out to the telephone in the lobby. Dave had followed him and listened. Jim had carried on a long conversation with somebody he called Brock. Dave hated being a rat, so he hadn't told his mother. He figured it was probably a toll call, and planned to check the telephone bill when it came.

The officer didn't pursue the interview any further, and departed.

Dave had kept his mouth shut about another matter which bugged him worse, and this was Jim's interest in Emily. When Jim had stayed with the Harrisons during the winter months he had liked Emily. Whenever he was having one of his running fits and had passed the Richter place he had stopped to kid with the Richter girls. Well, Emily was pretty then, but in a few short months she had really bloomed.

Dave noticed that Lew had a hard time keeping his eyes off her, and he saw how the guests watched as she moved around the dining room. With her eyes as blue as summer skies and her gold hair and her skin like pink velvet she was absolutely beautiful. Dave had happened to be looking, the first time Jim met her after he came back to Hobb Creek. Jim had been practically knocked out cold on the spot.

Now, every night Jim either drove her home or

walked her home, when she finished her work. He was always back within an hour. Dave knew because he kept tabs on the clock. What the others didn't seem to realize was that on Thursday, Emily's day off, Jim disappeared too.

The girl from town who substituted for her mentioned to Dave that Jim and Emily had been seen that Thursday at a roller-skating rink in Northford. Well, that wasn't exactly a crime, Dave supposed. He felt a surge of jealousy, wishing he could be the one to take Emily skating. Nevertheless, again he chose not to rat on Jim by repeating this bit of information to Beth.

He was mightily relieved, however, on the following Thursday, when Mr. and Mrs. Richter appeared at the inn. Lunch was over, and Dave and his mother were helping the substitute girl set up the tables for dinner. They looked up and there were the Richters in the lobby. Beth went to welcome them and Dave followed.

The Richters were plain-spoken people, which was why it was so easy to be friends with them. Mr. Richter came straight to the point, "Do you know where Jim is, Beth?"

"Why, yes," she said. "He suggested that he do the shopping today, to save me the trip, and he took the pickup truck. He had to go the farmers' market in Northford, and also to the wholesale meat locker, so I don't expect him back much before five o'clock."

"Emily went with him."

"Oh."

"Now, I'm not going to put Jim down because he's done time," Mr. Richter said, "but . . ."

Mrs. Richter took over. "Our Emily is very precious to us," she said. "Well, you can imagine. She's kind of pretty, and we're always fighting off the local boys. And she's eighteen, and according to standards nowadays that means she's entitled to manage her own life. But, and I hate to say this, we wish Jim hadn't come back. He's Joe Harrison's son but he isn't like any of the Harrisons, and we don't want to see our girl in trouble by him."

This was really laying it on the line. Dave's mother looked frightened. "I don't know what to do," she confessed. "Jim's good around the place, he works hard, he gets along well with the guests. He's acting as lifeguard at the beach, and the children are crazy about him. Dave and I don't want to take away his chance, maybe his last chance, to build a real life for himself."

"I can understand," Mrs. Richter said. "You're caught in the middle, Beth."

Dave heard a rumble of wheels and said, "The pickup's back."

He went out, to help unload. Jim was alone. They carried the cartons into the kitchen, and Miss Flint superintended stowing away the supplies.

Dave found it hard these days to talk to Jim about anything, even minor, ordinary matters. He couldn't bring himself to tell Jim, "The Richters are with Mom, and they don't want you to hang around with their daughter."

When the job was finished Dave went back to the lobby, but the Richters had left. His mother sat at a table in the dining room, folding paper napkins. "I'm going to have a talk with Jim, but I don't have the faintest idea what I'm going to say," she told Dave.

She did talk to Jim, late that night after she and Dave and Jim had made last rounds. A few guests sat on wicker chairs, enjoying the coolness and the moonlight on the lake. Miss Flint was snoring up a storm in her room above the inn kitchen. Beth poured milk for the boys and set out cookies and then came out with it. "Jim, the Richters were here today, and they're disturbed because you and Emily are seeing each other."

"Because I did time," Jim said, pushing away his milk.

"Yes." Beth didn't try to soften the one word.

"I'm not good enough for any nice girl."

"Well, Jim, they feel Emily's rather special."

"That's what I think too," Jim said. "Next Thursday, if you'll let me take the pickup, we want to drive to the shore and have a swim in the ocean and a picnic. I guess I have to ask you if I can have the day off. And then I plan to ask her father if she can go."

Dave's mind was wandering. Emily was a bright girl, so what could she see in Jim? Oh sure, he was well-built, good-looking. But when it came to brains, Jim wasn't in her league at all.

Beth ended the discussion by saying that they would talk about Jim's borrowing the pickup before next Thursday came around.

Dave wished he could feel better about Jim. But he tensed up when his brother was near. Much of the time he felt as though they were all sitting on top of a load of explosives or something.

Did Beth feel this way too? Nowadays she didn't seem easy with him either. She watched him, when he was near. Dave wished he could ask her how she really felt, but he couldn't. He was afraid he would have to admit to her, "I wish I loved my brother but I don't."

Maybe he did love Jim, though, Dave thought. Maybe all brothers felt this way, hostile and at the same time fond of each other.

All went well for a few days. Jim really worked hard at being friendly. He didn't push himself in but he was always there, being helpful to the guests. Beth had bought a badminton set, and he played badminton with anybody who wanted a game. He stayed close when the little kids were in the water, sitting on the dock with Lew but watching carefully. He lent a hand when their mothers and fathers were trying to teach them to swim. He cajoled money out of Beth to buy new records for the stereo, and there was always music in the main rooms.

Besides all this he kept up his end with the work. Miss Flint said truthfully there wasn't a lazy bone in his body. He helped take care of the vegetable garden. He mowed the grass, kept up the borders of ornamental bushes, arranged groups of chairs and tables on the lawn for the guests. He wouldn't allow Miss Flint to lift things and came at her call when she wanted supplies brought up from the inn's basement.

Maybe Jim hoped all this model behavior would get him his date with Emily, but it didn't turn out that way. Beth got up the courage to come right out with it. "Jim, I'm sorry, I can't go against the Richters, so I can't let you take the truck on Thursday. I've thought and thought about it, but I just can't see my way clear."

Dave was watching Jim's face. A smile like the

one he used to wear was plastered on Jim's handsome face, and he said, "That's okay, Mom." Dave went cold, though. Jim's eyes looked strange. An expression very like rage lurked in them.

Something happened on Tuesday night. Beth had gone to bed early with a headache and Dave too was in his room, working on a car model. This was the first time in weeks he had found a couple of free hours and wasn't too tired to fool around with his hobby. He could hear the music out front, where a few of the younger couples had pushed back the tables and were dancing in the dining room. Dave planned to go down at eleven, and probably Jim would join him, to check through the public rooms and make the rounds outside.

Dave heard a squeak; the kitchen door of the ell needed oiling. He glanced out his window and saw the white gleam of Jim's T-shirt. Was Jim going to try to sneak off in the pickup for a late date with Emily?

No, Dave saw him walking away from the inn. Headlights of a car parked at the main road end threw beams along the lane. Dave crept downstairs, then ran, following. He ducked behind a tree when he came near.

A man stood beside the car, his dim form barely visible. Dave heard Jim say, "Hey, Brock!" and the man answered, "Hello, Jimbo, long time no see." Jim got in the car and the two drove off.

Dave went back and got into bed, but he forced himself to stay awake. The illuminated face of his table clock gave him the time, two o'clock, three o'clock. It was half past three when he tensed, hearing the squeak of the kitchen door. Jim was back.

Dave was dying for sleep, but it didn't come. Should he face Jim in the morning with the fact that he knew Jim had gone off on some kind of a night adventure? He couldn't decide. The fact was, he was scared of a real showdown.

He was afraid he'd blurt out the truth, that he wished Jim would go away and stay away. Because then everybody would know what a lousy guy, what a cheap little guy Dave Harrison was, that he didn't want to share his home and his mother with his own half brother.

From that Dave's mind darted off on another tangent. He was thinking of something that had happened a couple of days ago. He and Lew were sitting at the end of the dock, getting their sneakers wet because the day was hot. Lew was contentedly watching his boats, dotted over the surface of the lake. He was counting up what tips he could expect, and he and Dave were talking about that when they heard a shot.

They listened hard. Nobody was supposed to be hunting, this time of year. A second shot reverberated from hill to hill and Dave said, "It's across the lake."

"Maybe some summer guy is target shooting," Lew suggested.

A third shot, echoed a few minutes later by a fourth, bounced off the hills. "That's not target shooting," Dave said. "The guy's moving toward the south end of the lake."

Lying in the dark Dave thought over the incident and decided, I'd better check Dad's revolver. How did anybody know what Jim did when he disappeared from the property for an hour or two? Why did Dave instinctively connect Jim with the shooting? He didn't know, except that these days he was growing more and more suspicious of Jim.

He finally dozed off. As usual the alarm clock blasted at half past six, and he groaned, longing to slip back into sleep. He couldn't do that because his mother depended on him. He sat up and scratched his head and remembered last night, and decided to check the revolver.

He did, the first chance he got. It was always kept in the locked drawer of the sideboard, and the key was kept under the kitchen towels in a drawer by the sink. The key was there but the gun was gone.

He had no choice: He had to tackle Jim directly about this, because only Jim, Beth, and Dave knew where the gun was kept. He found Jim in the garage, removing the mower from the tractor.

For a minute Dave watched him, wishing he had inherited Joe Harrison's size and strength, too. Jim handled the heavy machine as though it was a toy. Jim looked up and saw him and began telling him he planned to put on the sickle bar and cut the open fields south of the inn, because the guests' kids were afraid to walk there on account of snakes.

Dave wished he wasn't shaking and he wished he could think of a casual way to bring up the subject, but he couldn't. "Jim, the revolver's gone," he blurted.

"Is it? "Jim said. "Hand me that heavy wrench, kid."

Dave gave him the wrench. "So I want to know where it is," he said.

"Maybe it's in my room."

"Was it you who was shooting on the other side of the lake, a couple of days ago?"

"Maybe. Yes, I guess that was me."

Dave began to get angry. "So what were you shooting?"

"Vermin," Jim said. "That's what the fellers call it."

For a minute Dave was so shocked he couldn't speak. He went cold. Nothing in his past knowledge of Jim prepared him for this. Had Jim's stay in prison changed him so much? Then Dave went hot with rage. "What fellers?" he demanded.

"Well, like the guys I used to know in Hobb Creek, before I got sent to prison."

"What do you call vermin?"

"Woodchucks. Squirrels, things like that."

"I suppose you'd call an opossum vermin." Dave was thinking of the one that had lived in the tool drawer last winter.

"Yeah, I guess so."

"Dad never intended that gun should ever be used to kill with!" Dave shouted.

"You did," Jim said. "You killed a deer with it." Jim too was angry, and Dave realized that Jim was still hurt because of the way Dave had put him down and refused to give him the revolver that terrible day. "That was different," Dave stammered. "The deer was suffering."

Jim changed the subject. "You know that Bert Warden, the guy you had the trouble with? He's got another trapline down at the south end of the lake, on Sunset Point. I met him. He was having trouble with a raccoon in a trap, so I helped him."

"How did you help him?" Dave demanded.

"We clubbed it."

"You killed it! Why do you have to go along with somebody in a lousy deal like that? Suppose it was Herman, the one you used to have for a pet?"

"It couldn't be Herman. I bet Herman died a long time ago. Davey, what are you so mad about?"

Tears blinded Dave and he swung away. At the door of the garage he turned. "You put that gun back and don't you ever lay a finger on it again!" he shouted. Then he ran down the lane, away from home, trying to get hold of himself.

12

When he got back home, Lew was looking for him. They were supposed to hill up the corn in the garden patch that day. It was a hot job in the July sun and Lew didn't care to tackle it alone.

They worked for a while, hoeing the dirt up around the stalks. Finally Lew said, "Boy, you sure are a silent customer today."

"I know," Dave said. "I've got things on my mind. Maybe I'll tell you later."

He was trying to decide whether to spill the whole story to his mother. He checked at noon and again in midafternoon and the gun was still missing. He was getting more and more scared. Jim couldn't be trusted with possession of a lethal weapon like that .38. After he made a final check at dinner time and it still wasn't in the drawer, he found his mother in the kitchen helping Miss Flint, drew her into the inn pantry, and told her, "The gun's gone. Jim's got it."

"Are you sure?"

"I'm sure. He's the one who was shooting the other day, on the other side of the lake. He promised to put it back but he hasn't put it back."

"This is serious," she said. She asked Miss Flint to get the dinner on without her, and joined Dave in the ell. They searched everywhere to make sure Jim hadn't returned the gun to a different drawer. No, it was gone.

Beth's face was pale and determined. She sent Dave to make sure the pickup and the station wagon were in the garage. Both were there, so Jim had to be on the place. Unless he had simply walked off, taking the gun with him. They looked in Jim's room and saw that his clothes and his few personal belongings were there. "I hate to do this, it seems so sneaky," Beth said, but she resolutely began searching through Jim's possessions.

They didn't find the gun. They were just about to leave when Jim appeared in the door, and it seemed to Dave he loomed up about nine feet tall. "Are you looking for something, folks?" he asked.

"Yes," Beth said calmly, "your father's revolver. I want it, Jim. Right now."

He brought his hand around. "Here it is," he said. "I was putting it back, and I heard you in here."

Beth took the revolver, returned it to its drawer,

put the key in her pocket. "Let's sit down, boys," she said quietly, but Dave guessed that her knees felt as weak as his did.

They faced each other across the kitchen table. It took a long time, but they talked the whole situation through. Beth mentioned her worry that Jim was seeing Emily on the sly, and Dave brought up the incident of Jim's sneaking out in the middle of the night and going off in a car. Jim readily admitted he had met a prison pal named Brock Slate. Through the while interview his open face was expressionless.

Dave marveled at his mother's strength. She sat with folded hands, seeming steady as a rock. A silence fell. Finally Jim said, "Maybe I ought to go away."

"Yes, Jim," Beth said gently. "Maybe you ought to leave. I'm afraid we've reached the point where we just don't trust you."

"You could trust me if you tried!" Jim exclaimed.

Another silence fell. Dave couldn't break it, he couldn't think of one single thing to say, and they simply sat, waiting. Then Jim said, "I won't bother you anymore. I'll go tomorrow morning."

They listened while he telephoned his friend Brock and asked Brock to pick him up. Then the three went to their rooms.

◉

Dave could tell by the way his mother's bed creaked that she wasn't sleeping. He himself put in one of the worst nights of his entire life. What kind of a life would Jim walk into, when he left Journey's End? This was Dave's own brother they were pushing out of the house, the only brother he would ever have. It meant something that they shared the same father, it meant an awful lot.

A half dozen times Dave started to get up, to go to his mother and say, "Jim hasn't got any other place in the world. This is the only place he's got. Let's give him another chance. Maybe it'll work out." Each time, Dave stopped.

He stared at the ceiling, his arms folded under his head. Once he shot out of bed, thinking he smelled smoke. No, there wasn't any smoke. What was he afraid of? That Jim would turn mean and do something crazy like setting the place on fire?

No, Dave couldn't believe that. Just the same, he simply did not dare to fall asleep.

Dave and Beth were exhausted when they came down the next morning. Jim was packed and ready. Beth cooked a good breakfast for him. She gave him all the cash she had on hand, over a hundred dollars. Then they waited, and the waiting was intolerably painful. Finally Dave got up the courage to ask, "What will you do, Jim?"

"Oh, I'll get a job, I'll be okay," Jim said, feigning cheerfulness.

The honk of a horn rescued them. Jim kissed Beth and shook hands with Dave, saying, "So long, little brother," and grabbed his duffel bag and ran. Dave was afraid he might be crying, but no, they watched him greet his friend as he got into the car, and Jim seemed to be laughing.

That was a rough day. Miss Flint accepted the explanation that Jim had left to take another job. Lew was full of questions, and bugged Dave.

Emily was hurt. She asked Beth straight out, "Why did Jim go off without saying good-bye to me?" Beth was evasive and said something like, "There wasn't time," and Emily didn't buy that. She came as near being rude as it was possible for her to come; her attitude showed clearly she thought Beth had driven Jim away.

Finally Dave drew her aside. "Look, Em," he said, "none of this is Mom's fault. I should think you could see that Jim's not the kind who can settle down in one place and stay put, and keep out of trouble."

She turned on Dave and snapped at him. Then she apologized.

Dave and his mother just dragged through the day because they were exhausted from lack of sleep.

Also it was becoming clear that Jim had carried more of the work load than they had realized. "We'll have to hire somebody full time," Beth mentioned.

By the time they went to their quarters that evening, her face was drawn and lined; for the first time in his life Dave saw his mother looking old. "Dave, I've got a horrible feeling I've let your father down very badly," she admitted.

Dave protested that she hadn't let anybody down, but she went on, "I've told you how hard your father tried to get custody of Jim when he was small. Joe never stopped loving him and worrying about what was happening to him. And Dave, I know Jim loves you and I believe you love Jim."

Dave couldn't argue with that. There was nothing he could say. He was beginning to realize what a heavy load of regrets and sorrow people picked up as they went through life. He was picking up a few regrets himself. He heard her crying softly, alone in her room, and wanted to go to her, but what could he say?

He was feeling an awful sense of loss, as though there was a big hole in his life. Jim had said once he couldn't seem to hack it in the outside world. So where was Jim tonight? Where would he be tomorrow?

Life did get easier at Journey's End, though, as the days went on. They hired a senior high school boy, Benjy Sarker, who was glad to get a full-time job. He was good with motors, although not as good as Jim. He took over Jim's work, the mowing and keeping up the grounds, and also served as lifeguard when the little kids were on the beach.

Life was more peaceful, certainly. Dave put it into words. "When Jim was around it was like we were always waiting for the other shoe to drop," he told Beth.

"I'm not sure it's dropped yet," she said. "I keep remembering the second time he was arrested, when he took the car and drove off. I thought the shoe dropped then. I don't think we've heard it for the last time. I brace myself, whenever the telephone rings. And then I feel so ashamed of myself for worrying about us when I should be worrying about Jim. Oh dear! He's such a darling boy in so many ways!"

Finally the phone did ring one day, and it was Jim himself, not somebody calling with bad news. "Hey, folks!" he cried, sounding like his old, exuberant self. He had called because he wanted to let them know he was still in the land of the living. He had a job working at a McDonald's, helping in the kitchen, taking care of the grounds. He was bunking with Brock. Brock was a great guy, they'd like him if they knew him. Brock was working in a garage. Maybe they'd be moving on soon. Jim said to give his love to Emily and Lew and Miss Flint and keep some themselves.

He started to hang up. Then he said, "Dave, boy, I want to tell you I'm sorry about that raccoon."

"What raccoon?" Dave asked.

"The one I clobbered. You know, the one that pal of yours, Bert, caught in a trap."

Dave said an idiotic thing. "Well, we've all got to go sometime," he said.

"Yeah," Jim said. "So long, folks. I'll call you again."

After that call they felt easier about Jim. They found peaceful moments, like one evening when the long day's work was done and dusk came. Dave was down by the lake looking for a toy truck one of the kids had lost. The kid had cried at dinner, and Dave had promised to look for it. He found it in the grove of pines down by the water, half buried in dry needles.

His mother had seen the flashlight moving around, and joined him. "Thank heavens," she said. "The little boy was really upset."

Dave snapped off the light. This was a lovely spot, under the tall pines. He loved to come here, loved to breathe in the heavy pine smell. They stood there looking out over the calm lake, hearing the sounds of the inn behind them, music in the lobby, guests laughing and talking on the lawn. Dave snapped on the flashlight, and Beth touched his arm, and he looked where she pointed.

Two big, golden eyes were caught in the flashlight's beam, watching them from the bushes at the edge of the grove, too high for raccoon or opossum or rabbit, too low for deer. A fox? A bobcat? Beth's hand stopped Dave as he made a move to switch off the light. " 'Tiger, tiger, burning bright / In the forests of the night,' " she whispered, and went on reciting a poem.

Dave didn't understand the poem. "Except it isn't a tiger," he said.

"Let it go," she suggested. He snapped the light, snapped it back on, and in that instant the eyes had vanished. "I'd like to think it *was* a tiger," Beth said, laughing at herself.

August had come and the season was at its height. The rooms were full all the time, and they could have rented more. The word had gone far and wide that fishing at Enoch's Pond was the best in the state and that Journey's End offered comfort and fine food. The Harrisons and Emily and Miss Flint and Lew and Benjy were talking about opening all twenty-five rooms the following year.

Jim didn't call again, and it seemed as though he had dropped off the face of the earth. They rarely spoke of him; was it because they had secret hurts, like Emily's, or a sense of failure, like Beth's and Dave's? Anyway, life was definitely easier.

Dave hadn't been kidding, though, when he said he was waiting to hear the other shoe drop. He had an uneasy feeling he would be expecting that thud for the rest of his life.

And then it dropped. A car drove up the lane at midnight, and the slam of car doors woke Dave. His mother was stirring, and when he came out of his room she was buttoning her robe. They went downstairs.

Two men were at the door. Dave caught the smell of beer. "Hey, folks, I'm home!" Jim cried.

"Your bad penny is back," the other man added.

13

JIM INTRODUCED his companion. This Brock Slate was wiry, very tall, dark, and his eyes darted all around the kitchen. Maybe Jim was drunk but Dave doubted that Brock was. "Mom," Brock said. "That's what Jim sometimes calls you so I'll call you that too. Can we stay here tonight?"

Dave felt his mother's trembling. Neither of them knew what to do. "Well, I don't know," Beth said.

"We can both bunk in my room," Jim put in.

"I suppose it would be all right," Beth said reluctantly.

"Come on, Jimbo, show me where to put the car," Brock ordered.

The minute the men were gone Dave said, "Mom, I think we'd better call the police." Her safety was the thing that worried him most.

"No," she said. "Jim and his friend haven't done anything to be arrested for."

"I'm scared the cops are looking for them."

"Dave, we can't turn Jim in ——" It was too late to argue. The pair were back.

Dave realized by now that they weren't really drunk. Jim had brought in his old duffel bag, and he tossed it in the bedroom. "Mom, do you suppose you could fix us up some supper?" he asked.

"I suppose so," she said. "I have some hash I can heat up, and I'll fry some eggs. And then we'll all go to bed."

She took bowls from the refrigerator and started fixing the meal. Jim invited Dave to sit at the table with them. Dave had nothing to say, nothing at all; he couldn't manage to get out even the most casual remark. Jim asked how things were going and Dave said fine, and Jim asked who they'd hired in his place, and Dave croaked, "Benjy Sarker."

"How's he doing?" Jim asked.

"Okay."

"How's Lew?"

"Okay."

"How's ——" Jim began, and stopped, but Dave knew he was going to ask about Emily.

Beth interrupted this conversation by serving the food. Brock began shoveling his in fast, without a word, but Jim said, "Thanks, Mom." Dave was watching him and thought, "There isn't any real evil in Jim, he's just not too bright," and he was glad he hadn't called the police.

Beth took the dishes when they had finished, poured coffee, and said, trying to keep her voice confident, "Now Dave and I will go up and finish our night's sleep, and I'd suggest you do the same, boys."

Jim got to his feet. "Thanks for the supper, Mom," he said.

Beth and Dave went to their rooms, but paused in the hall. Beth was shaking with a real chill. "I wish I'd locked the door to the front of the inn," she whispered.

"I'll keep an eye on them through my ceiling hole," Dave whispered back. "What's the matter, Mom? You wouldn't let me call the police. I thought you thought it was okay."

"I was wrong. I'm afraid I'm always wrong, where Jim is concerned."

"You go to bed," Dave ordered. "I'll come and tell you if they start anything funny."

He was surprised, but she did as she was told. He heard the creak of her bed. He sat on his too, to make it creak, in case the men below were listening. Then he lay flat on the floor on his belly, his chin on his arms, surveying the kitchen.

The men kept their voices low. Brock lit a cigarette and asked if Jim thought the old lady had any beer, and Jim said no. Then Brock said, "Okay, where's this great .38 you were telling me about?"

Jim went straight to the towel drawer, found the key, unlocked the drawer in the sideboard. Dave silently cursed himself. Why hadn't he gotten around to hiding it in a different place?

"I see the kid is keeping it clean," Jim commented and passed the gun over to Brock.

Their voices were low, but Dave heard perfectly. Luckily they didn't know about the ceiling hole. Brock spun the chamber. "It's a beauty," he commented. "Where's the ammo?"

"They keep it in the same drawer." Jim found the box.

"Good, it's half full." Brock swiftly loaded the revolver, and the way he did it made Dave's heart lurch. This man knew guns, and he loved guns.

"Okay," Jim said. "Now let's get to sleep. We want to be out of here before they get up in the morning."

"I suppose," Brock said. Then he added, "Not so fast." He was looking around. "That TV is worth a hundred bucks."

"No," Jim said.

"How about a radio? Do they have a citizens' band?"

"No."

"How about silver? We can't take a lot of bulky stuff but we could peddle silver."

"They don't have any good stuff." Jim pulled open the drawers in the sideboard. "Here, you can see for yourself."

"Yeah," Brock said, "it's plate."

Jim knew that Beth had inherited from her mother a set of sterling, which was kept in flannel bags in the old chest in the corner. Jim wasn't saying anything about that. "Look," he said, "I told you about the gun and maybe I shouldn't have. But we're not taking anything else. These are my folks."

"So they're your folks, so why did they throw you out?"

"I was the one who blew it," Jim told him. "If I'd kept my nose clean and acted right, they would never have thrown me out."

Brock wasn't listening. He was walking around the room now. He took Beth's handbag from the doorknob where she always hung it. Jim protested, but Brock ignored him and turned the bag upside down on the table and pawed through the contents. He opened the wallet, riffled the bills. "Not bad," he said. "Forty bucks."

"We can't take her money!" Jim exclaimed.

Brock paid no attention. He paused in front of

154

the sideboard. "If they kept the gun locked in that drawer, maybe they keep some other good stuff there." When his hand came out it was holding a small, white, jeweler's box.

Dave almost cried out. Brock slipped Beth's sapphire ring on his finger, turned it so the diamonds sparkled. "Not bad at all," he said. "What's this?" He was examining Joe Harrison's Swiss wrist watch.

"That was my father's," Jim said. "Put it back. Put the ring back."

"So now the watch is yours. Take it, Jim boy."

"No!" Jim cried.

"Okay, if you don't want it." Brock slipped both the ring and the watch into his own pocket.

"Please, Brock, put the ring back," Jim begged, and he was sincerely begging. What the social worker at B.R.I. had said flashed through Dave's mind, that Jim was easily led by bad companions.

"Please," Jim said again.

"Why?" Brock demanded.

"Those things are Mom's."

"Don't be an ass all your life," Brock said coldly. "Now, Jim boy, we're going out to the front of this place, where the office is. Because if she keeps forty bucks in her pocketbook she probably keeps more in there. Come with me. I'm not going to leave you alone here. And then, buddy, we're clearing out. It's dark outdoors and I don't think the kid got a look at the car or the license plate. But maybe he did, maybe he's smarter than he seems to be."

Jim hesitated. "Come on, sonny!" Brock ordered sharply. Jim reluctantly followed his friend into the main inn.

Dave went to his mother. "Could you hear?" he whispered.

"I heard enough."

"I'm going down and call the police."

"No!" She clutched his arm. "They might come back. I'm desperately afraid of that Brock!"

It was lucky Dave didn't try it, because the men took only a few minutes. "Nice haul," Brock said in a low voice, stuffing bills into his wallet. Dave knew there were over two hundred dollars in the money box under the counter in the lobby. "Now we'll go," Brock added. "All set?"

"Listen, Brock, please be a nice guy, please put the ring back!" Jim sounded like a small boy, trying to wheedle his friend into doing the right thing.

"Don't be a bloody fool," Brock said. "You don't get anywhere acting like one of the straights."

He glanced around. "We cut the phone in the other room, so we'll cut this one, then we're all set."

Brock used his pocket knife and hacked the phone wire. "Come on, pal," he ordered. They tried to be quiet, but the TV set bumped as they carried it out the door.

Beth and Dave stayed upstairs and heard the car start, turn, and head down the lane. It picked up speed as it swung into the main road. "I'm going to the Richters and call the cops," Dave said, and swiftly pulled on pants and a shirt and sneakers.

His mother tried to stop him. "Dave, I'm afraid they'll come back and catch you! Let's wait until morning."

"And let them get clean away?" Dave abruptly left her.

He pedaled his bike fast the whole distance, and his anger must have pumped new strength into him because he wasn't even breathing hard when he flung himself onto the Richters' porch. It was a wonder he didn't shatter the glass in the door, he banged so hard. Lights went on all over the house.

He didn't stop to explain to Mrs. Richter, but the family followed and heard. The sergeant answered at the State Police barracks and he poured out the story. He couldn't give any description of the car except that it was big and dark and he thought that by the flickering glow of the taillight he had made out an *M* as the first letter of the license. Yes, it was an out-of-state license plate but he didn't know what state.

"We'll do our best, and I'll get it on the air right away, and I'll call Delaney and send him out to your place," the sergeant told him. "You're absolutely sure it was your brother Jim?"

"For crying out loud, I wish it wasn't Jim!" Dave shouted.

"All right, all right, sonny, take it easy," the sergeant ordered, and rang off.

Mr. Richter took Dave home and Mrs. Richter and Emily came along too. Beth had made coffee. She was holding up fine, although Dave could see her nerves were ready to snap. They were all gentle with Emily, who cried quietly.

The State Police car soon arrived. Officer Delaney took down their description of Brock and the list of what had been stolen. "Two hundred and forty in cash," he said, reading his notes. "A portable color TV, RCA. You haven't got the serial number? No, nobody thinks to make a note of that until the TV's stolen. A ring, sapphire surrounded by diamonds in yellow gold. A man's watch, Swiss make, yellow gold. Anything else?"

"The gun," Dave said.

"What gun?" Officer Delaney looked up.

"My dad's .38 revolver."

"Jim knew you had it?"

Dave looked at his mother and she answered, "Yes, Jim knew about the gun. That's the reason we asked him to leave this place, he was making too free and easy with it."

"What make?" Officer Delaney asked, his tone grim.

"Smith and Wesson," Dave told him.

"Ammo? Did they find any ammo?"

"Yes," Dave said, "the box was more than half full."

The phone was out of commission so the officer went to his car to contact the barracks. Beth followed him out, so Dave went too. The first thing Officer Delaney said into the mike was, "Two men, armed and dangerous."

"No!" Dave exclaimed. A sudden, absolute conviction made him say, "Maybe Brock is, but Jim's my brother and Jim isn't dangerous."

"Two, armed and dangerous," Officer Delaney repeated. "Brock Slate, tall, dark complexion, age about twenty-three. Boston accent. James Harrison, blond, over six feet, age about twenty, record grand larceny. I haven't got the other one's record but he

159

was a cellmate of Harrison's at the State prison. Car large, dark, first letter of out-of-state license possibly *M*." He listed the things that had been stolen.

He didn't linger after he finished. "You go in the house, ma'am, and take it easy," he advised. "I'll have a man sent to connect up your telephone. We'll get in touch as soon as anything develops."

Beth made one last appeal. "Please, won't you tell them to be careful with Jim? He's *not* dangerous."

"I know Jim too, and I wish I was as sure he's not dangerous," Officer Delaney told her.

"He's easily led. None of this was his idea."

Mr. Richter was listening and he grunted indignantly; he didn't share Beth's opinion that Jim was either dumb or innocent.

"He told his pal about the gun," the officer pointed out. "That's why they came here, isn't it? To get the gun? That's the impression I got from Dave's story. The rest of it, taking the other stuff, that was an afterthought."

"Jim didn't want to take the money. He tried to make Brock give back Mom's ring," Dave put in. "He was awful upset about that. Jim would never steal from us!"

"Maybe," Officer Delaney said. He got in his car and left.

There were still three hours to get through before morning. Mrs. Richter ordered Beth and Dave upstairs to bed, saying that if they didn't sleep they could at least rest. "We got a fair night's sleep before Dave banged on our door," she pointed out. "Pa and Em and I will be comfortable here in the kitchen until daylight."

Beth protested that she and Dave would be all right now. "We won't leave you here alone," Mrs. Richter said firmly.

The Harrisons did as they were told. Dave lay on his bed, but as soon as he tried to relax he started shaking with a hard chill.

The thing that stuck in his mind was the way Jim had pleaded like a little boy to make Brock give the ring back. Oh, Jim had been afraid of Brock, there was no doubt of that. And Dave remembered word-for-word Brock's answer, "Don't be a bloody fool. You don't get anywhere acting like one of the straights."

Dave stiffened, hearing a car in the lane. Mr. Richter, too, must have thought it might be Brock and Jim coming back, because he went to the door and shouted, "Who's there?"

"It's the telephone man," a calm voice answered. "You people are sure uptight. The police got me out of bed, they said you had to have phone service, so here I am."

Beth was stirring. Gray light was seeping in the window, and Dave realized with a heavy heart that another day had begun.

14

THE RICHTERS went home. The phone man mended the telephone wires and departed. Benjy arrived, bringing Lew. Miss Flint came down, and the boys pitched in to help start breakfast for the guests.

Beth was the last to appear, and Miss Flint exclaimed when she saw the black circles under Beth's eyes. They were all rehashing the events of the night, and Lew and Benjy were asking questions when the phone rang. Dave went to the reception desk to answer.

He couldn't believe his ears — it was Jim. "Where are you?" Dave shouted.

"I'll tell you. We didn't get very far, we had a flat tire and no spare. Dave —"

"I'll call Mom," Dave interrupted.

"No, there isn't time, Jim said. "Brock's in the men's room, but I'm scared he'll catch me calling you. Tell the cops to come and get the stuff."

163

"Where, where?" Dave cried.

"The sign says 'Eagle Diner'."

"But where is it?"

"I don't know. We went through Northford, and then we had the flat tire and walked to this place. I've got to go. So long, kid."

"Hey, Jim, take care of yourself!" Dave yelled.

"Yeah."

"Jim, keep the faith!"

"Yeah, you too, little brother." Jim added hastily, "I can see Brock, he's come out of the john. He shouldn't have took Mom's ring!" Jim shouted, and slammed down the phone.

The barracks number was scrawled on a pad, and Dave called the sergeant. The sergeant said there was an Eagle Diner south of Northford and they had a cruiser working the state road in that area. Then Dave went to tell his mother.

For the first time Beth fell to pieces. She sobbed, and kept crying, "I've got to go!" The others said she shouldn't go, it was police business, but Dave understood. She and Dave had been through too much with Jim for her to stay home waiting for good news or bad news or whatever kind of news they were going to get. "All right, Mom, we'll go," he said, "but we'll let Benjy do the driving. All right?"

164

Lew wanted to come too but Dave said no, Lew would have to stay and help Miss Flint and Emily look after the inn. Benjy got the car and they set off.

Dave didn't know Benjy well, but today Benjy seemed steady and dependable. Beth sat up front with him, and urged him to speed up. She seemed to have some desperate sense of urgency, as though if they got there in time they could prevent something terrible from happening.

They reached Hobb Creek and swung onto the state road; then Benjy obeyed Beth and stepped on the gas, cutting in and out of the line of cars. The traffic was heavy at this time in the morning. "Look, Benjy, a couple of minutes isn't going to make all that difference," Dave said. "Let's keep it down, okay?" He himself wasn't in any great hurry. He didn't know why, but he just didn't want to get there.

"I guess you're right, Dave," Benjy said, and slowed.

In the outskirts of Northford they got tangled up in worse traffic, near a factory. Dave glanced at his watch. An hour had passed since they left home. Whatever was going to happen had happened by now. Had the cops nabbed Jim and Brock?

They were watching for a sign and Benjy spotted one, "Eagle Diner, quarter mile ahead." After that they didn't watch because suddenly they were going bumper to bumper. A cop was directing traffic ahead, waving cars onto a side road. They recognized Officer Delaney.

He waved them to the right too, but Beth said, "No," and Benjy stopped. Officer Delaney came over, angry about the delay. He leaned in the car window and said, "Oh, Mrs. Harrison," and his face changed and he said, "You can go on, I guess. And I'm sorry."

Benjy drove on, and they didn't have time to wonder what Officer Delaney was sorry about. They rounded a curve and there was the diner. Police cars were all over the place. An ambulance was parked, its red roof light circling. In the middle of the highway a blanket was spread over something on the concrete. Benjy said, "I've got an awful feeling," and then shut up and stopped the car.

An officer rushed over to them, waving his arms to make them get out of there. "I'm Mrs. Harrison," Beth called.

He came closer. "Oh," he said, "you're Mrs. Harrison. You shouldn't be here, ma'am."

"Where is Lieutenant Thorne?"

"He's inside. I'll get him."

Left alone for a minute, Beth turned around and grabbed Dave's hand. They stared straight ahead, careful not to look at what was on the road. Dave's throat closed, he felt he was strangling. He knew. Did his mother know too?

Lieutenant Thorne came out to the car quickly. "Yes," he said, his voice careful and quiet, "it's Jim. Suppose you come inside, Mrs. Harrison. Dave too. You stay here, son," he told Benjy.

The diner was empty except for a few men at the counter. They stood up when the lieutenant ordered, "Somebody get this lady a chair. This is the boy's mother."

"No, not really, I'm Jim's stepmother," Beth said, and Dave glanced at her face, astonished by her calm. "Dave is Jim's brother. Would you please tell us what happened? And where is Brock?"

"He didn't get far," the lieutenant said. "The men found him in the patch of woods out back of this place. He'd thrown away the gun, but the men will find it. He's on his way to the prison at Hampton. He needs maximum security.

"Mrs. Harrison," the lieutenant went on, "this is Arnold Hopson, who owns this place, and Steve, the cook, who witnessed the whole incident. We're just getting the facts now."

The proprietor started right in, eager to tell his story. "Ma'am, I was telling them how these two came in and sat down at the counter, and I didn't like the look of them so I kept an eye on them. The one

167

they call Brock, he asked about a garage, and I told him, and he used the pay phone outside to make a call, I guess he asked them to bring a new tire, because their front right was all tore up. Then they ordered breakfast.

"I poured them their coffee. Then this Brock, he went in the john, and the one they call Jim, he asked for a dime, quick, and I gave it to him. He went outside, and I could see he was talking to somebody on the phone, but he kept looking back at the diner.

"He spotted Brock, and he came out of that phone booth real quick, but this Brock, he was swearing and he rushed out and met Jim on the steps. They yelled at each other and Brock yelled, 'You finked!' And there right in front of my eyes he whipped this big revolver out of the top of his pants, it looked like a .38, I know guns ——"

"Joe's revolver," Beth said. "Oh my God." She clutched Dave's hand so tight he cried out with the pain.

"Yes, ma'am," the proprietor said. "Well, this Jim, he turned around and ran out to the main road, and a car was coming and he waved his arms to flag it down, but Brock, he stood right there on my diner steps and took aim. His face was swelled up and red, he was so mad, but he took aim careful and slow, and fired. The boy went down, dropped like a stone. I knew he was dead."

There was a flurry of activity because Beth sagged in her chair, her face chalky white. Dave got his arms around her and somebody brought a glass of water. After a minute she whispered, "I'm all right."

"I shouldn't have let you hear it this way," Lieutenant Thorne said, his face full of concern.

"No, it's best this way, straight out," Beth said.

"But now I think you ought to go home. We'll be in touch with you."

Beth stood up, and an officer steadied her elbow, and the lieutenant came out with them. Outside in the parking lot, Beth stopped. "What about the — the —"

"Jim's body," the lieutenant said quickly. "It'll be taken to an undertaker in Northford. Do you wish to claim it, Mrs. Harrison?"

"Yes," she said. "He's a member of our family."

The lieutenant took something from his pocket. "Everything will be returned to you, what they stole, the gun and so forth, but they're State's evidence and have to be held until after the trial ——"

"No, not the gun!" Beth said fiercely. "It has to be smashed up, so no one can use it ever again."

"Well, these you'll want, I'm sure," Lieutenant Thorne said, and put the sapphire ring and the watch in her hand. "We'd rather not keep them at the barracks. They will stay in your custody."

Dave spoke for the first time since they had arrived. "That's why Jim called," he said. "That's what he couldn't stand, Brock's taking the ring."

Lieutenant Thorne helped Beth into the car. Dave got into the front seat with her because they needed each other's nearness and comfort. The ambulance was gone with its heavy burden, the traffic was moving, only a couple of police cars were left. There was nothing to indicate that a tragedy had happened. It occurred to Dave, "It's like Jim has been swept under the rug."

Was his mother thinking along the same lines? "He'll be buried in the Harrison plot, near your father," she said in a low voice.

Dave thought Benjy required some kind of an explanation, and began, "Brock shot Jim."

"I know," Benjy said. "One of the cops told me."

Beth was talking again. "Courage is a funny thing," she said. "Well, your dad had it, Davey. You know how brave he was, when he was so sick. He had a saying and it was a good one, 'It isn't life that matters, it's the courage you bring to it.'

170

Jim — his came in a sudden rush." She choked, stopped.

Dave cleared his throat. "And that's what we'll remember about Jim," he said in a tight, high voice.

After that, they rode the rest of the way home to Journey's End in silence.

Miss Flint came out to meet them. She tenderly took charge of Dave's mother, shepherded her into the ell kitchen, and sat her down and talked soothingly while she made a pot of tea.

Benjy told Dave he'd take over the job of telling Lew and Emily. Nobody needed Dave right now. He had to get away from the house, and he went outside.

His feet led him down the slope to the grove of pines. He walked around in circles, scuffing pine needles, his mind in a turmoil. He couldn't bear to think of Jim right now, that was too hard, so he was remembering the night he had dug up the trap here, and flung it in the lake.

Although there was a hush within the grove he heard voices all around, small children shrieking in the water, their mothers calling orders. Benjy must have finished telling Lew and Emily, because Dave heard the roar of the power mower. Somewhere out on the lake a fisherman let out a whoop, meaning he had caught a big one.

Soon everyone would know. Then, Dave supposed, there would be a hush over the place. Would the guests leave?

It was so quiet and it smelled so wonderful, there under the tall pines. Dave shielded his eyes, staring out over Enoch's Pond. The little red rowboats shimmered as though in a mirage. The sky was a blue, cloudless dome and the far hills shimmered too, blue in the summer heat. The scene was so beautiful. So why did there have to be so much ugliness?

Big, blond Jim, he wasn't ugly. What happens to people when they're dead, Dave wondered. Where was Jim now?

He remembered something Mrs. Richter had said, when Jim came home that first time from B.R.I. Some people had criticized Beth for taking him in, but Mrs. Richter had said, "You have no choice, Beth. Blood's thicker than water." That meant family ties, blood ties of family, and Jim was Dave's half brother.

The monstrousness of death was more than Dave could accept this morning and he told himself, "Jim *is* my brother." But he had to accept the truth at last and he said to himself, "Jim *was* my brother." And with that Dave began to cry softly, sobbing and hiccupping into his handkerchief.

It took a long time for the tears to pass, but finally he felt empty. He blew his nose hard. He stared dry-eyed out over the lake, and he said in a low voice, "So long, Jim."

He couldn't stay here in the grove, hidden away. His mother would miss him and know he needed comforting, and would come looking for him.

He started up the slope toward the inn, trying to leave Jim behind him, in the grove, but he couldn't do it. Benjy was mowing, over beyond the badminton court, but he wished it was Jim who sat proudly astride that big mower. He had adored that power mower. Jim and his loud laugh and his broad, happy face.

Dave went up the steps of the inn. The guests were assembling in the lobby, waiting for the wide doors to open for lunch, and there was the usual talking and laughter. They didn't know yet. Dave slipped through, and crossed the dining room to the kitchen.

Emily was shouldering a heavy tray. Her face was composed and she had fresh lipstick on but her eyes were dull. Emily didn't know it but today she seemed like Dave's sister. Right this moment, Dave felt as though he had to embrace everybody, as though everybody in the world was his brother or sister. He didn't dare not to. He couldn't afford to make that mistake ever again, as long as he lived.

He gave Emily a ragged sort of a smile and said, "I'll take that, Em," and carried the heavy tray into the cheerful dining room.